# DREAMS OF THE VENGEFUL

A MASSACRED DREAMS PROLOGUE

ADELAIDE FORREST

Cover Design by Adelaide Forrest

Proofreading by Light Hand Editing

Created with Vellum

# ABOUT DREAMS OF THE VENGEFUL

***Our love was written in blood, but our dream was born from death.***

*Once upon a time, I had it all.*

Born heir apparent to one of the Six Families,
I was destined for greatness.
Wealth and power were in my blood, and
sweet Thalia was one more means to an end.

Until they banished me from the watchful city,
stripping me of everything I possessed,
my name, my home, all I'd come to hold dear,
including the girl who was to be my wife.

*Now the day has come to take back what's mine.*

The girl is no longer a promise I need to protect,
but a woman who I plan to devour.
Wealth and power are in my blood, and

sweet Thalia may very well be my end.

*Dreams of the Vengeful is the prologue to the Massacred Dreams series and is a dark mafia romance that ends with a cliffhanger. It contains elements that may be triggering to some readers, including depictions of violence, situations involving dubious consent, graphic language, and references to child abuse.*

# PART I

BEFORE

# 1

## CALIX

Twenty years prior.

The air inside the Karras home turned suffocating as soon as I scrawled my signature on the page, on the contract that bound me to a future no boy would choose for himself. Just like my father, Origen Karras built his empire on lies and suffering, on business arrangements and on the arrogance of the figurehead who sat behind a desk, striving to unite the six families for his own selfish greed.

Anyone could see it if they merely looked hard enough, seeing past the proper veneer of the image he tried to present. Glimpsing the monster residing beneath his skin.

I stumbled out the back door of the house, my lungs heaving with the ridiculousness of it all. The arranged marriage that loomed on the distant horizon, to a tiny slip of a girl I'd only seen in passing, sent me spiraling out of the stuffy estate and seeking fresh air.

The girl was five years old, far too young to already contemplate which monster would share her bed when she was old enough to breed, and yet that was precisely what a group of grown men had chosen to do on a sunny Spring afternoon.

At thirteen, I'd already lost my virginity and appreciated what girls my own age could do with their changing bodies. The thought of that with a girl less than half my age made my skin crawl.

I leaned against the railing at the edge of the elaborate wood deck, my eyes catching on the bright green blades of grass that had only sprouted from the frozen ground weeks prior. As my gaze dragged up to the expanse of yard at the back of the estate, my focus narrowed on the form of a young girl twirling between the gardens of narcissus that her mother must have been fond of to have so much growing on the property.

She looked at me, a smile on her heart-shaped face as she spun and completely oblivious to the contract that had been signed only moments before. The ink of my name probably hadn't even dried on the page as of yet, as our fathers and her brother toasted to the agreement.

To cementing the alliance between our families despite her mother's obvious desire to stall it. But there was no stopping tradition and there would be nothing to save little Thalia from becoming mine after she became a woman.

As a kindness to her mother, they'd agreed Thalia didn't need to know until she was old enough to understand. She could have her childhood and enjoy the promise of freedom when she would come of age.

Even if it was a lie.

My legs guided me toward her, closing the distance between us even though I knew I should stay away. To get close to her and never tell her the truth of what was to come felt like a cruelty she didn't deserve, and nothing about the five-year-old girl would last until our marriage. She'd be a new person by the time she became mine.

Our lives dictated that.

She continued spinning until dizziness consumed her, falling to her back in the grass and staining her yellow sundress. My mother would have disapproved greatly, because young ladies should always present themselves properly. Not be stained with grass after rolling in the dirt.

She stared up at the sky, the sun sparkling off the unique amber of her eyes—completely oblivious to my approach. "Shouldn't you be inside?" I asked, stuffing my hands into the pockets of the suit pants my father made me wear.

Already a man ready to take the city by storm in his mind, I was no longer a boy.

She startled, pressing a hand to her chest as she flung up to sit and that distinctive stare landed on mine. She squinted at me, fixating on something on my face as she tilted her head to the side. "Why?" She rolled her eyes and shrugged, dropping back to the grass as if she couldn't be bothered to concern herself with what the adults might be doing inside.

Despite my better instincts, I moved closer and risked my mother's wrath to sit on the ground next to her. Kicking my legs out in front of me and feeling strangely awkward, I picked at the blades of grass beneath my hands. "That's a good question," I admitted and huffed a laugh.

"Being inside is so boring. Out here, I don't have to be so quiet." Her face pinched together, not quite pretty enough to be adorable. Her eyes were too big for her face, her lips puffy, and her ears had an odd sort of point at the top like she was something straight from a fantasy book. Her face was intriguing, her features bright as she turned a smile my way, but between her odd face and the tiny frame that looked far too young for a five-year-old, no one would ever call Thalia Karras pretty.

Perhaps that would change by the time we married.

I swallowed back the despair that tried to settle over me, knowing that the future waiting for us wasn't one either of us would have chosen for ourselves, yet still trapped by the forces working to drive us together.

"What do you like to do?" I asked, thinking maybe I could send her gifts. Get to know her a little, bit by bit, without ever truly being a part of her life. Just enough so it wouldn't seem so agonizingly painful when the contract came due and her life became mine.

"Draw, but Daddy doesn't like it. I like to draw flowers, but the colors are always wrong, and—" She cut off suddenly as if she'd realized she'd said something she shouldn't.

With a swallow, she sat up, curling her arms around herself protectively. "You're five. Flowers can be any color you want," I said in an attempt to comfort whatever nervousness had settled over her.

"Can they be black and white?" she asked, her eyes turning hopeful as she leveled me with that wide-eyed stare.

"Wouldn't you rather they be pink?" I asked, furrowing my brow. What little girl painted black flowers?

The hope faded from her eyes as she pushed herself to standing once more, leaving me staring after her from the ground. "I have to go."

I moved to follow, taking up a slow walk at her side as her little legs worked to make her way back to the house. She was so painfully thin that it seemed as if each step required too much energy. Still, there was a stern determination on her face that didn't belong on anyone her age.

As if she had to do it for herself, or the consequences

would be dire. "What color flowers do you like best?" I asked, resolving to send her some that she could draw.

She paused, her steps halting as she hit me with a concerned stare. "I'm not supposed to talk about it," she said, biting that too-large bottom lip and staring nervously toward the house. Her eyes darted from window to window, swallowing when she found no one watching us.

"About your favorite color flower?" I asked, grinning down at her in my confusion. She was such an odd child, and if her parents truly forbid her from talking about the flowers, then I couldn't imagine what kind of life she had with them.

"I don't know," she answered. "I can't see them." She picked up her steps, quickening her pace as her lungs heaved with exertion. I was half tempted to lift her into my arms, knowing her tiny frame couldn't weigh much.

"Flowers?" I asked, laughing at the ridiculousness of the notion. I'd only just seen her twirling in the fields surrounded by narcissus and never harming a single flower.

"Colors," she whispered as she reached the back door, taking the handle in her grip. She turned back to me, her eyes silently pleading to keep her secret. Whatever she saw on my face must have reassured her, because she nodded once and pursed her lips thoughtfully.

Looking far too old for her body and for her age, she turned the handle and swept into the house. She was gone by the time I followed, disappearing like a ghost in the wind.

Like she'd never been meant to exist at all.

# 2

## THALIA

*Ten months later.*

The knuckles of my left hand ached as I washed the blood away. My split skin moved as I flexed my fingers, watching the dark stained water swirl down the drain. My mother hovered in the doorway, her face pinched as she watched me. "You must remember to use your right hand, Thalia."

"I know, Mommy," I said, turning to stare up at her face. It had been almost a year since I'd made the silly mistake of telling the boy I didn't know my secret.

I hadn't made that mistake twice. Even though he hadn't told on me, nobody else made me want to trust them as much as the boy who'd sat with me in the grass and didn't look at me like I was a broken doll.

Mommy's light hair gleamed in the overhead light as she stepped in to help me clean the sink basin. It was far easier for her to spot the red stains than it was for me to tell them apart from the dark spots of the marble.

Daddy hated when I used my left hand, because "proper girls" were right-handed. Proper girls didn't stop to think about which hand they should grab their fork with at the dinner table. Even a moment of hesitation meant Daddy reached across and struck my left hand that he sat next to at the table for dinner every night.

"These will scar," Mommy said, grasping my hand in her grip and studying the wounds that never healed. Every strike, every lesson, reopened the injury until my left hand always hurt.

I thought that was the point. In his words, Daddy would beat me into being right-handed if he had to.

"Miss Thalia, Calix Regas is asking after you," one of the housekeepers said as she poked her head into the open bathroom door. Her eyes narrowed in on the injury I tucked behind my back in shame, a scowl pinching her lips together. The shadows under her eyes grew worse by the day, as if she couldn't stomach working for our family.

I knew it would only be a short while before she too left.

They always did.

"Who?" I asked, turning my eyes to my mother who set to straightening my dress. To studying the fabric and checking for bloodstains. It wouldn't be the first time that I'd wiped my injury onto my dress, but I did my best not to.

Daddy didn't like it.

"He's the heir to one of the six families," my mother answered, fluffing up my wavy hair. She took my right hand in her grip, tugging me out of the bathroom and pasting that fast, easy smile that came so naturally to her on her face. I envied her ability to smile even when she wasn't happy. She said I'd learn in time.

We stepped out into the dining room where my father stood beside the already cleared table, his eyes angry when he turned his attention to us. I swallowed back my nerves, letting my mother lead me to the boy standing beside him.

The same boy who'd sat in the field with me and kept my secret. The same one who I knew I shouldn't trust, but something in his eyes made me wish I could.

"Calix," my mother said as he leaned forward and kissed her cheek. He was just a boy, years older than me for sure, but he couldn't have been old enough to be as tall as he already was.

"Mrs. Karras," he said politely. He nodded to my father, who bit his cheek in displeasure but stepped over to my mother and took her hand. He guided her out of the room, leaving me alone with the boy when I knew it couldn't be what my father wanted.

I wasn't supposed to be alone with boys.

"I brought you something," he said, squatting down so that he was my height. He held out a single light rose, and I took the stem in hand, noting that he'd trimmed the thorns off. I drew it to my nose, inhaling the uniquely sweet smell as I bit my lip.

"Why are you here?" I asked, wincing as I thought of how my father would scold me for being so rude. It wasn't normal for a teenage boy to want to spend time with a child.

"A little birdy told me that tomorrow is your birthday," he said, standing and reaching into his back pocket. The box was small enough that he had tucked it away, but curiosity got the best of me as I reached out to take it from him.

"What is it?" I asked as I pulled the lid off. Inside the heart-shaped box were six little plastic pockets, each with a rounded ball nestled inside.

His, *Calix's*, eyes narrowed as he watched me lift one into my hand. "It's chocolate, Little One," he said, grinning at the flush that warmed my cheeks. Nobody ever called me anything aside from my name.

Not even my mother.

"Have you never had chocolate?" he asked, taking the one from my hand and holding it out for me to take a bite out of. I hesitated, staring at him for a moment before I leaned forward and bit into the soft chocolate. My eyes widened as the sweetness of it exploded over my tongue, forcing myself to chew politely even though I wanted to snatch the other half out of his hand.

"No," I said softly before I leaned in to eat the other half. He chuckled as he drew his hand away and wiped the excess chocolate from his skin onto a napkin from the table. "It's yummy."

"I'll bring you more the next time I come to see you. Would you like that?" he asked. I tilted my head to the side, still wondering what could possess him to want to spend time with me and why my father would allow it.

Even the girls at school didn't want to be around me.

"Okay," I said warily as I put the lid on the chocolates and placed them on the table delicately. Without knowing how long it would be before his next visit, I felt the need to make them last.

To save them for the bad days.

I drew the rose to my nose once more, inhaling to fill the quiet that claimed the room after my admission. He didn't seem to know what to say, which I guessed was normal considering our age difference. He pushed to his feet, towering over me once more as he glanced to the door. "Do you like it?" he asked, shrugging his shoulders as if he couldn't decide why he cared.

"It's pretty, and it smells nice. Thank you," I said.

"It's pink," he answered, as if that meant anything to me. I'd never seen the color pink. There was nothing to connect to that word. "I thought it would be nice to have something different than all the narcissus flowers in the yard."

"I like the narcissus," I said defensively. "They're mostly white. I don't—" I paused, sinking my teeth into the corner of my mouth on the inside.

"You don't what?" he asked, leaning forward to tuck my hair behind my ear. His fingers hovered at the odd point at the tip, but where others made fun of me and called me names, he gave a slight smile.

As if maybe they were cute and not freakish.

"I don't feel like I'm missing out. Narcissus is pretty even though it's just white. I don't need to see color to love them," I said.

He froze solid, staring at the rose in my hand and gave me a kind smile. "I'll bring you a white rose next time, *λουλούδι μου,*" he said. "How does that sound?"

"It sounds perfect," I said, smiling up at him. He nodded once, turning for the door without so much as a goodbye and leaving me to stare after him as he stepped out into the night.

Grabbing the box of chocolates off the table, I tucked it under my arm and made my way for the stairs to go up to my room. My father stepped out of my parents' bedroom, eyeing the rose and the chocolates in my grip with distaste. A scowl transformed his face, the only warning before he reached forward and snatched the rose from my hand. Throwing it to the floor, he crushed it with his foot while I pursed my lips to keep from crying.

The chocolates were torn from my arm after and tossed to the side for the housekeepers to deal with. "Daddy!" I protested finally, reaching out to them with my left hand. He smacked his hand down on top of mine, the slap echoing through the hallway as I cradled my injured hand to my chest and stared up at him.

"Did you invite him here, girl?" he grumbled.

"No," I denied shaking my head furiously. He nodded once, moving toward the bedroom he shared with my mother. In the silence that followed, her pained whimpers trailed out through the open door.

"You'd better hope I don't discover you're lying," he barked, making me jolt in place as I sniffled back my tears. Stepping into the bedroom, he closed the door to cut off the sound of my mother's pain.

It was never enough.

# 3

## CALIX

Thad pulled up at the curb to the private all-girls academy, and I peered out the window as we waited for the school to let out. Cars and personal drivers all waited to grab their charges, nannies filling the space outside the building. "I'll be right back," I said to my driver.

Hauling open my door, I stepped out into the brisk air. Spring hadn't yet arrived, the last lingering effects of frost keeping flowers from blooming.

I wondered if Thalia still twirled in the yard when she wasn't surrounded by a black and white garden of flowers. The innocence of her youth was something I'd never known something I couldn't remember ever having myself.

Such were the differences between the expectations put on male heirs and daughters, whose sole purpose would be to be wed and bred, I supposed. While I hadn't said anything, I'd seen the injuries on her knuckles. The scrapes and torn flesh, surrounded by various stages of healing that hinted at repeated abuse.

While I might not care for Thalia in the traditional sense like a husband might his wife, she was still *to be* mine to care for. Something in the young girl made me want to protect her, even if she hadn't been contracted to be mine one day. Those wide amber eyes just made me want to ensure that no harm came to her.

That innocence needed to be protected for as long as possible.

To ask the questions that needed answering, I would have to catch her without the threat of her father looming over her. I needed her to tell me how she came to be injured.

Then I would have to convince my father to back me up when I stepped in on her behalf. He wouldn't give the first shit that a girl was being abused, so it would take me some time to find a way. A bargain would need to be struck, and I hated to think of what I would need to sign over to my bastard of a father to protect Thalia.

Still, sometimes things needed to be done.

I watched as the girls finally emerged from the front of the building, chattering excitedly as they hurried through the cold to get to the nannies and parents waiting for them. Thalia was impossible to spot in the crowd, so painfully small for her age that I almost didn't see her when she stepped out at the back of the group. With her eyes to the ground in front of her, she didn't so much as glance at any of the other girls as she passed.

The innocent but lively and curious girl I'd seen in the two times I interacted with her in the last year was nowhere to be found, drowned out by the sadness and dread on her face. Stepping toward the front of the gate, I waited for her to look up and see me waiting. For that moment where her excitement would peek out from under the quiet illusion she wore.

I didn't get the impression many people seemed to care about her thoughts or feelings. It bothered me more than it should that this girl I barely knew was silenced by the people in her life.

She never saw the two girls reach out for her, each touching a hand to a shoulder blade and shoving her forward. Thalia's hands struck the pavement as she caught herself, and her face twisted with pain when one of the girls nudged her with a shoe and shoved her to her back. She stood over Thalia, leaning in to hiss something at her with a cruel sneer on her face.

I was already moving, closing the distance between us to stand with a foot to either side of Thalia's head. The other girl looked up at me, blanching when she saw the raw fury on my face. Thalia was small. She was awkward, and she suffered from color blindness. I couldn't begin to imagine what that was like when so many people depended on color to identify and describe *everything.*

The last thing she needed was to be bullied by some snot-nosed kids who thought their shit didn't stink.

"Get the fuck away from her," I growled, my lips pulling back to reveal my teeth. Rage filled me as I bent down and grasped Thalia under her arms, hauling her to her feet in front of me and taking the backpack off her shoulders to carry for her.

It weighed almost as much as she did.

"You are going to forget that Thalia exists. If I *ever* hear you've been bothering her again, I will find you and I will make your life a living hell, you little shits," I growled, watching as the girls nodded quickly and raced off. "Are you okay?" I asked, turning my attention back to Thalia. She nodded, keeping her eyes on the ground. "Little One?" I reached out to touch her hand with one of mine, growling when she flinched back as if I might hit her.

Any doubt I might've had that her injured hand wasn't the result of an accident fled in that moment.

"I will never hurt you," I told her firmly, squatting down and being reminded yet again of just how small she was. I grasped her hands in mine and turned them over, staring down at the raw skin where she'd caught the pavement and the spots of blood that peppered her skin.

"I'm fine," she said, snatching her hands away defiantly. I released her right but kept my grip strong on her left, twisting it to stare at her knuckles pointedly as I raised an eyebrow at her.

"These didn't happen today," I said, scowling down at the scarring around her knuckles "Who did this?"

"None of your business," she muttered, tugging until I had no choice but to release her. She grabbed the strap of her backpack and tried to yank it off my shoulder, but only glared at me when she couldn't. Huffing a breath of annoyance, she crossed her arms over her chest. Even in her warm jacket, her arms were far too slim, and her knees were knobby where they peeked out from her skirt.

"Let's get you to the car," I said with a sigh. "Eventually, you'll tell me who hurt you."

"It doesn't matter," she said, breathing in a more subdued way. As if she truly believed that nothing and no one could change anything about her treatment.

I'd move the earth for what was mine, and, like it or not, Thalia was my responsibility.

We stopped at the car waiting for her, and I glared at the driver. I contemplated giving him an order that Thalia wasn't to be harmed, but I refrained. I'd tell her father my fucking self. I imagined most teenage boys were afraid of the great Origen Karras.

There was nothing I hated more than a bully who

picked on the weak, and it took a special kind of asshole to bully his own daughter. I swore on my life there'd be a special place in hell with his name on it.

"What color are your eyes?" Thalia asked suddenly, tilting her head to the side as that curiosity leaked back into her face.

I blinked back my impending rage, staring down at her as a smile curved my lips up. "Gray." She grinned at me, all full lips and big teeth, instantly reminding me of why she liked white flowers.

She didn't have to feel like she was missing out on the color with my eyes being what they were. For one rare moment, she could stare at something and know she saw it for what it was.

## 4

## CALIX

I strode up to the Karras household with my father's men at my back. Even though he'd neglected to show his face for the girl who would one day be his daughter-in-law, he hadn't allowed me to come unaccompanied either.

Our lawyer glanced around the ornate entryway of the expensive home as we stepped in through the iron doorways. It was early enough that Thalia was still at school, so thankfully she wouldn't need to be subjected to the details of our arranged marriage.

If I had it my way, she wouldn't need to know the truth until it came time to arrange our children's marriages. I could protect her from the knowledge that she'd been sold off to strengthen a weakening alliance, all part of the six Greek families' plan to connect us all intricately over the course of three generations.

The woman who'd allowed us into the manor turned, making her way toward the back of the house and the office where I'd signed the contract nearly a year earlier. Following at her heels, I drew myself up and squared my shoulders for the argument I knew was coming. Thalia's father wasn't likely to take kindly to me telling him how to parent his own child.

I didn't give the first shit.

The office door was open and I didn't hesitate to step through it. Our lawyer, an aging man with stark white hair, named Erasmos, followed me inside silently while my father's men lingered just outside the doorway. Origen Karras sat behind the desk, not a single concern on his tight expression as he watched me stroll into the room and take the seat across from him. Erasmos dropped the briefcase on the desk in front of me, opening it before stepping out of the way.

"And what's this?" Origen asked, his eyes narrowing in on the stack of papers I pulled from the case.

The updated contract was stark white against the deep wood of his desk, and I found myself considering it from Thalia's point of view. Black and white and shades of grey: her world existed without warmth.

In more ways than one.

I turned to the pages where we'd added the addendum about her care and wellbeing until she came of age and became mine. Looking at him directly, I tapped the tabbed section where he'd need to read. "After visiting with Thalia yesterday, I'd like to make an update to our arrangement."

His eyes turned glacial as he glared at me, not even bothering to look down at the papers. "I assure you, whatever the girl has done can be remedied by the time she's eighteen. Her behavior is a work in progress," he said.

My nostrils flared as I fought back the rising anger that came with his automatic assumption that Thalia had done something wrong, when it had undoubtedly been him in the wrong.

I quirked a brow, swallowing past the lump in my throat as I leaned back in my seat and turned my attention toward Erasmos as he spoke. "The updated section proclaims that Thalia Karras will not be harmed in *any* manner while under your care. She is to be given a safe and comfortable home in which to grow into the woman she will be, and all decisions regarding her discipline or education will need to be approved by Calix Regas from this moment forward. As you do not seem particularly inclined to childrearing without harming Thalia, Calix will be an active participant in her childhood with weekly visitation."

"You would have her weak and pathetic? A sniveling and imperfect mess of a girl is all you'll achieve by coddling her. There are things you do not know about her that need to be corrected, foolish boy," Origen snapped, jabbing his pointer finger into the contract. "This means nothing if I do not sign."

"I know that she is colorblind," I said, my fingers biting into the arms of the chair as I pulled myself forward. "Unlike you, that does not matter to me."

He paused, his jaw clenching in shock as he glanced toward the door. Even though it was too early for her to be home, his fists clenched as if he had the driving desire to strike Thalia for admitting the truth to me. "It is a weakness. A genetic anomaly that should not exist. If I had known she would be deformed in this way, I would have aborted her before she could ever shame us. She *will* learn to function without revealing it to those around her," Origen warned, skimming through the contract.

"Then she will do that without your abuse," I returned with a warning growl. "You have far more to lose from this contract falling through than I do. What do you think the rest of the families will think if you allow all their plans to fail purely because you insist on hitting what is meant to be mine? I have seen the scars and fresh wounds on her hand with my own eyes. What purpose could that possibly serve that is so important to you?"

"The brat is left handed, if you must know. She ends up with ink and lead all over her hand when she writes. It's unacceptable for a girl of her stature," he said, shrugging his shoulders as he sat back in his seat. As if the repeated and casual abuse of his own flesh and blood for such an insignificant reason mattered little.

I stilled my body, leaning forward to lift a pen off the desk and set it on top of the contract. "You strike your daughter for writing with her left hand?"

"I strike her for *using* her left hand for anything. Eventually, she'll associate using it with pain and stop altogether." A cruel grin twisted his lips as he watched my anger rise.

One day, I'd kill him for the cruelty he'd shown a tiny slip of a girl he was meant to care for.

The Families be damned.

"Very well. I suppose I'll just have to notify the others of your lack of cooperation," I said, sliding my chair out from beneath me.

"You already signed the contract, boy. She's yours, whether I abuse her or not. The only requirement is that she be kept virginal for you to bleed on your wedding night. You've shown your hand and your own weakness. I should send her to your marriage bed scarred and broken for your threats," he said, standing as well.

"Do you think I would come here without having some assurance the Families will see it my way? All of the contracts have been updated to match the one you're looking at. Everyone else is in agreement, since they don't beat their own daughters. You'll be the sole man to dismantle the plans for combining the Families." I shrugged, knowing he was trapped as his face dropped with the reality of what was coming. "What do you think they'd do with that? After years of negotiations, I think they might do *anything* it takes to make sure you aren't a problem anymore."

"You *will* regret the day you decided to toy with grown men," Origen snarled, but he dropped his hand to the pen and contract. "And what will you have to show for it? A colorblind bitch of a wife who doesn't know her place. Congratulations." He scrawled his signature on the bottom of the contract where I'd already signed, letting Erasmos scoop it into his briefcase once he was done.

"My visits will be a surprise for a while. Until I'm confident my expectations are being met. I'm sure you understand," I said with a hard smile, turning back for the door.

I knew Origen would try to get even, but at least Thalia would be safe. I'd find a way to deal with her father eventually.

# 5

## CALIX

*One year later.*

Thalia grinned as she raced down the stairs, the sound of her tiny feet thumping against each step in her haste to make her way to me. Her mother stood at the top of the stairs, a rare, small smile on her face as she watched her daughter in a moment of happiness.

Those moments were so rare for Thalia and her mother, because even requiring that she not be physically harmed didn't mean I could control the mood of her home.

Her father was a tyrant, pushing his daughter toward perfection in a way that no seven-year-old girl should have to be. The aging and increasing tension on her mother, Neri's, face led me to believe that she'd taken the brunt of Origen's inability to punish his daughter.

I chose to think that she would welcome that, given it meant her daughter had been freed from the abuse. Any true mother would.

Thalia's small figure connected with my body as she flung herself at me at the bottom of the stairs. Her face pressed into my diaphragm as she tilted up to look at me. "What have you brought me today?" she asked excitedly.

A grin tugged my lips despite myself, the sight of her white teeth peeking out from her too big lips always bringing a rare moment of light to the life I led. Training to become the next head of the Regas family was all consuming, bringing me to places I never wanted to go.

In the time since Thalia had entered my life, I'd killed my first man. I'd tortured and bled and maimed countless other men in the name of the six families. Somehow, she still smiled up at me like I hung the moon and stars in the night sky and gave her light in the darkness.

"Let's go outside, Little One," I teased, nodding my head to the back doors so that we could go sit amongst the narcissus flowers. The garden was still her favorite place to chat with me, where the prying eyes of her father and his men weren't so noticeable and the ears were more distant.

"Fine," she said, sticking her tongue out at me. I let her take my hand and guide me through the house, her mother's watchful eyes fading from view. Jeno stood with his arms crossed over his chest at the back door, blocking the path with a harsh set to his jaw.

Considering we were the same age, I wasn't sure why he thought he could intimidate me. Everything he'd done and learned to become, so had I.

"Move," I ordered, raising my brow. I didn't care that it was his home and his sister who I let take me to the privacy of the outdoors, not when I had the other families on my side.

"It's fucked up that you're spending all this time with her, you know," Jeno said. "Why not just wait until she's older?"

"I'll be right out, *λουλούδι μου*," I said, nodding my head and sending Thalia outside on her own. She looked back at me nervously before shrugging her shoulders and tugging the door open as she maneuvered her way past her brother.

She sprawled on the grass between the flower beds in the distance, the taller grass of the field enveloping her as she stared up at the sky. "The next time you make a comment that alludes to the contract, I'll feed you to my dogs," I snapped, turning a glare to Jeno. He paled briefly, his face twisting with fury as he tried to recover from the threat.

"What fucking difference does it make?" he asked. "It's part of life for her."

"She doesn't need to know that until she's older, and if you care about your sister at all you'll make sure she doesn't. She has the opportunity to be innocent for a few years before the bullshit of our lives corrupts her. Don't you think she deserves that?" I asked, shaking my head at him. He didn't seem to care one way or another what happened to his sister, and I couldn't help but wonder why it seemed like the ones who were given such a gift never realized what they had. I shoved past him, leaving him to stare after me as I set to appreciating the light he'd been given.

Our relationship might become different as she grew, but for the time being I was her protector and the only person in her life who spoiled her.

She sat up as I approached, her dark hair spilling over her shoulders and the sunshine making her amber eyes stand out against the deep olive of her skin. "Well, what did you bring?" she asked, picking at the blades of grass under her legs.

"What makes you think I brought you anything?" I teased, taking up a seat in the grass directly across from her.

"You *always* bring me something." She giggled, holding

out a hand expectantly with a smug expression. Rolling my eyes dramatically, I reached into the pocket of my jacket and pulled out the chocolate chip cookie I'd snuck in for her.

I had no doubt her father knew about my tendency to bring her sweets, but the glee on her face as she dug into it was worth every bit of the wrath I might incur.

"How was school?" I asked as she took a bite of the cookie. She chewed, her little face twisting with a groan of happiness as she swallowed down the bite.

"Good," she said evasively. As far as I'd known, the girls at school hadn't given her any trouble since I threatened them, but she largely went ignored.

I guessed it was better than being bullied.

"What's a contract for marriage?" she asked, taking another bite of her cookie while I coughed to cover up the surge of rage inside me. If Jeno had told her, I would fucking kill him with my bare hands.

"Where did you hear that?" I asked, trying to suppress my initial response. Maybe it was innocent and meant nothing.

"Girls at school," she said, raising an eyebrow and seeing far too much for her age. "Missy Galanis said her father signed her contract for marriage to Stephen Lykaios yesterday."

I heaved out a sigh of relief, handing her the napkin from my pocket to wipe her chocolate-covered fingers on. She wrapped her arms around herself, shivering lightly in the chill air.

I slipped my jacket off my shoulders and wrapped it around hers. "Some of the families believe in using marriage as a business agreement. Instead of marrying for love like in your fairytales, they marry for money or power and it's usually decided when the girl is young."

"Eew. Stephen is like *old*," she complained. Even though he was only a half a dozen years older than me, the unfortunate reality was that made him twenty-one when Missy was only seven.

"I agree," I said, leaning back to stare at the clouds.

"Will that happen to me? A contract for marriage?" she asked, crinkling her nose, but the shadows in her amber eyes weren't playful. Thalia knew far more than she let on, and while she might not know for sure that my place in her life was similar, she had to know that the day would come.

"No, Little One," I said, my soul withering with the lie as soon as it formed on my tongue. One day, I knew I would regret the words, but for now the most important thing was preserving the innocence of her childhood. "I won't let your father sell you off to someone who doesn't care for you." The addition eased the sting, because I did care for her.

Even if it wasn't in the way I should care for my wife.

She nodded, the light returning to her eyes. "Promise?"

I nodded, wishing it was a word that I could keep. She deserved to marry a man she loved one day. Instead she'd be stuck with me.

I gave her the only words I could, sealing our fate with more lies built on childish dreams that had been massacred before they could ever flourish. "I promise."

# 6

## THALIA

*One year later.*

I smiled as I hurried down the stairs as quickly as I could, my left hand gliding over the bannister. As I rounded the corner toward the entryway, I was shocked to see my father standing in the doorway and looking at me with the cruel smirk he often gave my mother.

I sucked back my concern, knowing that the moment Calix had become my friend was the day my father's corrections ceased. We'd never spoken of it, but I knew he'd done something.

What a teenage boy could threaten the head of the Karras family with, I didn't even want to know.

"Come, Thalia," my father said, reaching out a hand to stroke over the top of my hair in a mockery of everything that was gentle about Calix.

"Where's Calix?" I asked, flinching away from his touch. He snatched my wrist in his hand, his fingers bruising as he gripped me tightly. His knuckles were stained dark and wet, the skin torn open. "Where is he?!" I yelled when he didn't answer, planting my feet as he dragged me out the front door. My heart sped, looking everywhere for Calix. He'd never once kept me waiting when he promised to visit. My father's car waited at the top of the driveway, his personal driver holding the backseat door open. My father shoved me in and climbed in beside me, making me turn wide eyes to him.

"You'll see him soon enough," he said, adjusting the sleeves of his jacket. Dressed from head to toe in black, he looked so different without the shock of a white dress shirt peeking out on his chest.

"Is he okay?" I asked, swallowing back the tears I knew would only anger him more. He hated Calix in a way that I wouldn't put it past my father to get rid of him at the first chance he got.

"Soon enough, everything will be exactly as it should. You can take comfort in the fact that you will not be punished for the mistakes of others," he said, glancing at me briefly before turning his attention back to the window. "But there will be a lesson to learn today. I hope you are smart enough to pay attention, my darling daughter," he said, staring out the window. He didn't look at me as he spoke the words, and dread gathered in my belly. His lessons always hurt, even when he'd stopped hitting me.

The streets of Chestnut Hill faded as we left the affluent neighborhood my family called home. We kept going and going until industrial buildings claimed the roads, and we made our way around the back of an old warehouse. Most of the buildings still seemed to be functioning, but despite the heavily armed security guarding the one in front of us, it didn't seem to be used by anyone recently.

My father stepped out of the car once it pulled to a stop,

nodding to me until I followed him out. He remained silent as he walked through the doors one of his men pulled open for us, letting me trail behind him even though all I wanted to do was run.

To find Calix and get out while I could.

He guided me through the main space of the building, the empty structure feeling cold. Even compared to the coolness of our home, something about it left me with a sense of dread.

Death clung to the walls. Death was on every surface and in the air, as if it was imprinted into the building itself and would never be clean. A graveyard with walls.

The doors at the back of the room opened and my father stepped through them. I hesitated at the sound of cheering voices coming from inside the new room. One of my father's men prodded me between the shoulders until I kept moving forward.

Men stood in a circle at the center of the enormous room, blocking my view of whatever might be in the middle. As my father reached them, they parted to allow him through. My feet dragged as I forced myself closer, needing to see whatever kind of Hell he'd brought me to see.

It was a punishment undoubtedly, for growing closer with Calix and not keeping him at an appropriate distance. Girls like me weren't allowed to have friends, especially not boys.

Not when my father said my allegiance would belong to my husband one day without question.

"Daddy?" I whispered, stepping up behind him. I hated the name every time I said it, knowing he'd never done anything to deserve it, but his insistence kept me from calling him anything else even as I shook with fear of what was coming. He moved to the side, allowing me to see into the pit in front of him. Metal plates lined the walls around the hole in the concrete, leaving them with nothing but a hole where the floor must have been at one point in time. It was huge, with a dozen people standing below and plenty of space to move around.

There were bodies littering what looked like sand on the ground, and I swallowed back my rising nausea as I realized the woman kneeling at the center of all of it with her head hung was my mother.

"Mommy!" I called, watching as her body twitched but she didn't raise her head to look at me. My father's hand grasped my dress around the shoulders, lifting me from the ground as my eyes connected with Calix's in horrified shock. He knelt on the ground in front of my father's men, his father and the men I recognized that worked their family's security watching in the background with their heads hung low.

Dark stains covered their clothes. Their faces. I knew even without the shock of color that it was blood.

The unmoving bodies littering the ground around the pit left no doubt to that.

My father tossed me into the pit, my hands and knees landing awkwardly in the sand as the tiny grains dug into my skin. Calix's eyes were wide as he shoved to his feet to reach me, grunting as someone wrenched his arms behind his back and secured them with rope while I pushed myself up to stand.

"She has *nothing* to do with this," Calix growled, struggling against the person holding him. His father knelt next to him, his beaten and bruised face a mirror of my father's torn up knuckles. Calix's bare chest was crisscrossed with bleeding wounds, one of his cheeks marked with a gash that would scar.

He'd always been inhumanly beautiful. From the moment I'd first seen him, I'd wondered how it was possible for a boy to be so pretty. The cuts on his chest and his face changed him, as well as the savage snarl on his face that I'd only ever seen when the girls at school pushed me years before. At his side was a blade, a sword, as if he'd dropped it when he hadn't had any other choice.

I spun, my eyes sliding over the wall at my back and the weapons lining it. My history lessons flashed in my memory. My father jumped into the pit at my side, chuckling and grabbing a fistful of my hair. He wrenched my head back while Calix yelled his protest. "Leave her alone!"

"Do you like ο λάκκος, my daughter?" he asked, his voice harsh. "This is where we settle our disputes with fire and blood. This is where decisions are made and the future is shaped."

"It's a gladiator ring," I wheezed, bringing my hands up to grasp at his hand. The blood coating his skin from whatever fight he'd been a part of made my hands slick, slipping along his and unable to find a grip.

"Good, Thalia. The Italians may be useless in most ways, but at least in this they offered something of value. An entertaining way to kill your enemies and fight for power."

"What did she do?" I asked, nodding my head, as much as I could, to where my mom still knelt in the sand.

"She allowed another man to touch her. My *wife* let Eugene Regas inside her, when her body belongs to me alone." I didn't understand the words, not fully, but I knew enough to know that a woman belonged to her husband.

My mother would never have taken such a risk. Not with the way my father beat her for everything she did wrong. He loosened his grip on my hair, tossing me to the side until I fell to the sand.

"Let her death be a lesson to you, so that you never forget your place and what happens when a woman disobeys her husband."

# 7

## CALIX

Origen left Thalia in the sand, making his way to his wife. Neri didn't lift her head, keeping her face to the ground until he touched her chin with mocking gentleness. He lifted her face until she blinked up at him blankly, as if she'd already withered and died.

As if watching the butchering of my father's men had killed what remained of her soul that Origen himself hadn't beaten out of her years prior.

Thalia's father's fist struck her mother across the cheek. Blood sprayed from her lip, staining the sand as she fell to her side. "Mommy!" Thalia screamed, lunging forward as if she might try to intervene.

I pushed to stand from my knees, desperate to keep Thalia from interfering. There was no telling what her father would do if she got in the way, no reason to believe he would treat his daughter with any semblance of kindness considering what she would see in a few moments.

She shouldn't have been there at all. Only men were allowed inside ο λάκκος, except for the rare occasion where a woman's infraction was severe enough to require more than one of the six families. My father being foolish enough to fuck Karras' wife qualified.

Rough hands snatched me around the rope at my wrist, wrenching me back to the sand. Thalia's brother, Jeno, stepped off the spot where he'd lurked by the wall, wrapping his arms around Thalia, restraining his sister as he watched his father strike his mother over and over until little remained of what had once been a beautiful face.

"Daddy, stop!" Thalia screamed, the shrillness of her voice echoing off the walls of the pit. The other families watched without a trace of emotion on their face, no concern for the fact that they'd only just years ago moved to protect a child from her abusive father. My own father's mistake had changed the tides of power, shifting it out from under me before I was old enough to shield Thalia from the consequences.

With her mother gone, what would my father's punishment be?

"Make him stop!" Thalia snarled, turning in Jeno's arms to push at his chest.

He shushed her, his voice oddly gentle. I barely heard it over their father's savage roar as he stepped up from his wife's limp body. Her lungs filled with air in a ragged breath as she turned to stare at her daughter. "Close your eyes, Thalia," she murmured, using all the strength she had to warn her daughter of what was coming.

Origen grasped one of the axes hanging on the walls, hefting the heavy weapon into his arms and moving back toward Neri's half-dead body where she lay in the sand. I lunged again, struggling against the hands holding me still. A fist connected with the side of my face, splitting the wound on my cheekbone open further and sending me stumbling forward until sand grated against my other cheek. Thalia's struggles increased as she watched her father stare down at her mother coldly, tears streaming steadily down her cheeks. "No!" she screamed.

"Close your eyes, λουλούδι μου," I said, my mouth moving against the abrasive surface of the sand. Thalia's tear-filled eyes found mine, her face twisting in horror. She was too young to understand, but just old enough to know what was coming.

To know she'd never see her mother again, and that her final memory of her would be one filled with the shadows of blood in her mind.

Her lip trembled as she stared at me, her eyes shuddering closed slowly so she wouldn't have to witness the death of the only person she loved. Jeno moved to step away, to drag her further from the carnage that would be her mother's death, but Origen didn't bother to wait.

He swung the axe down. The sound of the freshly sharpened blade slicing through flesh echoed through the pit as it embedded in the sand beneath Neri's body.

Thalia whimpered as blood splashed onto her bare legs, the liquid trickling down over the skin of her shins. Jeno swayed her back and forth lightly, a rare moment of affection that I'd never seen in all the times I'd watched him belittle or ignore his baby sister. Her eyes stayed clenched closed, waiting for the order from me. I knew without a doubt that Thalia wouldn't open her eyes until I told her it was okay.

Perhaps her mother wasn't the only person she loved after all, in the way a girl loved her protector.

Two of Origen's men stepped forward, grabbing Neri's corpse by the ankles and dragging her through the sand as the bodies of our men were disposed of in the same way.

They'd be brought to το νεκροταφείο. The graveyard where those who died in the arena were left to rot.

There would be no tombstone. There would be no place to mourn.

Just countless bodies decaying in the catacombs beneath the building.

Only when Neri's body was dropped through the hole at the edge of the pit and added to the pile of dead did I speak to Thalia. "It's okay now, Thalia," I murmured, watching as the four other heads of family lined up at the top of the pit. Origen hiked the axe up onto his shoulder, waiting for the moment when he was given permission to kill my father for his betrayal of what all the families held dear.

Marriage was sacred. Above all else.

"Eugene Regas, you have been accused of betraying our ideals and taking another man's wife to your bed. What do you have to say to the accusations?" the head of the Hasapis family said, staring my father down.

"Well technically I didn't take her to a bed at all. We never made it that far," my father sniped like the idiot he was.

Theodore Hasapis ground his teeth, glaring at him. "But you admit to defiling her marriage?"

"I don't think you'd have permitted my men to be slaughtered if you thought otherwise."

"Then you leave us no choice. We have determined that the Regas family will be exiled from Philadelphia. We care not where you go, but you are henceforth banished from the families," Theodore declared/ordered.

Thalia's father dropped the axe to the sand, his jaw clenching as he undoubtedly wanted to argue against the sentence.

My father's death would have been preferable for all

involved, leaving me to run the Regas family with him gone. Thalia would have remained protected. But with me banished from the city....

"We are not all to blame for the actions of one fool. Would you truly punish an entire bloodline for the sins of one?" I asked. My father turned his shocked expression toward me, but there was only one thought racing through my mind.

Protecting Thalia. No matter the cost.

"A rotten apple creates rotten seeds, and we cannot allow the disease of the Regas family to spread. You will leave the city immediately, and all contracts and business deals will be severed."

Thalia sobbed against her brother's grip as my father and what remained of his men were hauled to their feet. The man at my back tried to lift me, but I hunkered down and made my body as heavy as I possibly could.

I wouldn't leave her, not knowing that she'd have no one to defend her against Origen.

Thalia screamed out as her father's man drew a knife and pressed it to my throat. I swallowed against it, holding her eyes with mine and silently willing her to stay still. "Please no," she begged, shoving at her brother's arms until her father approached the two of them. “You can’t!” He took Thalia out of Jeno's grasp, twisting her arm behind her back until she cried out in pain.

"Get up, boy," Origen ordered. "We both know you're leaving the city one way or another."

"No," I spat, not daring to take my eyes off his. I might not have been big enough to truly fight for her, not compared to the men standing around and the sentries waiting to take me away from her.

But if nothing else, Thalia would know that I fought to

stay with her. That I'd cared enough to protect her with my own life.

"Get him out of my sight," Theodore said, waving a hand. Another man came up to me as the original sheathed his knife, his fist colliding with my face and assaulting me with a wave of pain. Another followed immediately, the pain inside my skull thundering as the blows kept coming.

Unconsciousness crept in alongside the sound of Thalia's screams. With the final realization of just how gravely I'd failed her, black consumed me, drawing me to a place where nothing hurt.

Only my heart.

# PART II

## AFTER

# 8

## THALIA

*Twelve years later.*

My pencil scratched at the page carefully, methodically outlining the details of the narcissus flowers woven into Persephone's hair. Lifting my left hand up from the page, I studied the wisps of smoke floating around Hades' beautiful face. Touching the side of my palm to the page, I smudged the lines until I was happy with the way the shading blended together.

He was bathed in darkness, hidden in the shadows with only light eyes and the subtle features of his fierce snarl peeking down at the lightness of Persephone. With her white hair and fair skin, the lighting seemed to make her sparkle. I dropped my pencil to the page, heaving out a sigh as I leaned forward and draped myself over my desk.

In just a few minutes, I'd have to tuck the sketch away from prying eyes.

I leaned over the drawing, smiling down at it. A moment later, the cane sliced through the air, the sound always so similar to the memory of my father's axe. To the thudding of it striking the sand after severing my mother's head from her body.

I might not have seen it, but even after more than a decade, that *sound* was firmly trapped in my memories.

Pain exploded across my back, old scars rising to ache with the injury I'd suffered through far too many times to count. "You're slouching," Lydia reprimanded as I smoothed my back to ramrod straight instinctively. My stepmother moved through the room silently, leaning against the edge of my desk and pursing her lips at the stain of lead on my hand.

Her cane tapped against the scars on the back of my left-hand knuckles, the skin warming instantly under her attention. "Your father won't be pleased to see you've been disobeying him again," she tutted. With a frustrated shake of her head that shook her light hair from side to side, she heaved a sigh. It wasn't often that she caught me drawing, not when I did everything within my power to keep it a secret.

I knew the consequences should my father discover I wasted time on such a frivolous activity that a woman of my stature shouldn't partake in. But the day had been long. The wait had been exhausting.

The sun had set hours before, leaving me to wonder just how long it could take for such a choice to be made. "He called. He'll be home soon," Lydia said. I nodded, keeping my expression carefully blank.

Emotions were for the weak. Love was a lie. Perfection was demanded.

Emptiness was my closest companion, and I'd long since accepted its place in my life. There was only one person who mattered to me. One who I would do whatever it took to protect. Even allow myself to be forced into a loveless marriage that was to be determined by a trial by combat. A barbaric way to determine who would earn the right to marry the eldest Karras girl.

"Is Malva asleep yet?" I asked Lydia, turning my eyes to stare into the empty fireplace in the corner of my bedroom.

"She finally drifted off about an hour ago," she said, a hint of warmth creeping into her voice. Despite her willingness to show me cruelty according to my father's rules, Lydia loved my half-sister with all that remained of her cold, cruel heart.

I nodded, drawing in a deep breath before I shoved my chair out and strolled into my bathroom. I scrubbed my hands raw, furiously removing all traces of my sketching from my skin. "He expects you to be waiting in his office when he returns," Lydia said, clearing her throat before she ducked out of the bedroom. I heaved a sigh of relief once she was gone, turning my eyes up to look in the mirror as my wet hands clutched the edge of the counter.

In two months, I would be married. I didn't even know the name of the groom, only that he would be an heir to one of the other four remaining families. In the days, weeks, and years leading up to the spectacle that my father found so hilarious, not one of my potential husbands had bothered to get to know me.

They hadn't done more than give me a glance-over at parties and determine that I'd grown up well before moving about their business. I'd given them the saccharine smile that had been forced into my muscle memory, all the while wishing I could go back to being the runt of a child that nobody bothered with.

Scrawny had grown into lithe limbs and a too-thin body

that was often painful to maintain. High cheekbones and wide upturned "amber" eyes made me look ethereal according to Lydia. An odd sort of beauty that required a second look to truly appreciate.

Because the first look was just odd and flawed, and I had the "type of beauty that took time to appreciate."

Drying my hands with the towel, I stepped away from the vanity and made my way into my room. Tucking the drawing with the others in the alcove in my closet, I made my way out into the hallway. With calm, measured steps and a carefully straight back, I held my head high as I passed my father's men, Leon and Peter. They'd been there the day my mother was murdered, and I hadn't been able to look them in the eye after watching them restrain Calix so he couldn't get to me and take me with him.

I'd have gladly gone, and I'd waited for the day when he'd sneak back into the city to rescue me from what he had to know was a horrible life. A mother, dead and murdered. A father who wanted nothing more than to hurt me to spite both her and Calix.

I'd have been better off bleeding on the sand of ο λάκκος than living the life he'd left me to.

But Calix never came back for me.

Peter slid his gaze down my body, lingering on the swell of my breasts in the dress Lydia had laid out for me that morning. I ignored him, turning the corner and descending the stairs as my hand ran over the railing.

My breath caught with panic, and I snapped my hand off the bannister as quickly as I'd set it there. My father didn't wait at the bottom of the stairs, and there was no cold smirk on his face to haunt me. But knowing he was at ο λάκκος haunted me. Nothing would change the fact that my future husband wielded a weapon in much the same way, bleeding men and fighting for the right to wed me like I was some prize and not just a broken doll.

Like I would be anything more than another expendable toy to sit on the shelf.

I turned the corner at the bottom of the stairs, making my way for my father's office at the back of the house. The door was open, the first sign that I'd taken too long before coming down.

It wouldn't please him, but I had to hope he'd had time to wash the blood from his hands and face before I would have to look at him. But I found as I stepped into the room there wasn't a speck of shadowed grey on his suit or his skin, because he'd had no need to fight.

He owned the prize the others wanted.

I stepped in front of his desk, hanging my head and dropping my eyes to my feet while I waited for him to speak. He sucked back another sip of his scotch before he stood, stepping around the desk to stand beside me. Leaning against the desk and crossing his ankles, he waited for me to flinch as he reached out a hand toward my face.

But there was no fear left in my body, no attempt to protect myself against the inevitable.

"Good girl," my father chuckled, touching my chin and turning my face until I looked over at him. "They fought hard for you."

I said nothing, allowing Origen to work through whatever grand speech he had planned for me. He loved nothing in this world except to hear himself talk.

He nodded, pursing his lips and moving away when he didn't get the affected reaction he wanted from me. "You're to marry Damianos Hasapis," he said finally, dropping into the seat behind his desk. "You should be pleased with that arrangement, I think."

I blinked once, the only sign that I'd even heard his words. I didn't know what I'd ever done to give him the impression that I had opinions of the men who might be my husband.

It mattered little to me since they were all the same. A symptom of the archaic traditions that ran rampant in the families and needed to be dismantled from the inside out before Malva could suffer the same fate. "He would like to spend some time with you before the wedding. He wants you to be comfortable with him and to understand that he intends to treat you well." My father scoffed his disapproval, rolling his eyes as if it was a ridiculous notion. "God help me, but I cannot seem to escape insufferable fools who would treat you like a precious gem. Tell me, what exactly have you done to earn such treatment?" he asked. "Besides becoming mute as well as half fucking blind."

"You've made it very clear that I serve one purpose, and it is not to be heard. I'm uncertain why you want me to speak if you don't wish to hear me, Father," I said, keeping my voice as neutral as the empty expression on my face.

"Even when you say everything right, you somehow manage to make me want to smack the smartass right out of you," he grunted, huffing a laugh as he waved his hand to dismiss me. "At least I won't have to deal with you for much longer."

I took the dismissal for what it was, turning on my heel, anxious to make my way to the relative sanctuary of my bedroom without another word. There was no lock on my door, nothing to keep me safe from him if he decided he wanted to invade my space. But Origen didn't seek me out. If he needed me, he'd summon me like a dog.

"Thalia?" he called. I paused, turning my head to look at him over my shoulder as rage gleamed in his eyes. "Try not to do anything stupid. I would hate for you to end up like your mother." I swallowed against the reminder, nodding my head briefly and shoving down the pain.

I lived my life by a very simple set of rules.

The first was to never let them see you bleed.

# 9

## CALIX

I marched through the house, my feet carrying me to the open-space living room. Rafael sat at the kitchen island, typing away at something on his laptop with that grim look on his face. He knew what was coming.

He'd always known since the moment my father had left my broken body on Miguel Ibarra's doorstep.

I'd fought like hell to stay with Thalia, to protect her from the fate I knew would come in my absence. She'd be punished for the fact that I dared to defy Origen Karras, and she'd suffer for getting close to me.

"Who?" he asked, not bothering to look up from his laptop.

My ally in Philadelphia had called me as soon as the victor was declared, but it had been a long, painful wait before I knew the name of the man I would slaughter. The man who tried to take what was mine.

"Damianos Hasapis," I growled. The son of the man who had sentenced me to banishment alongside my father.

The son of the man who had taken everything from me.

Rafael nodded, finally glancing up. "That's good. His

father needed to die regardless of the son's involvement in this. Perhaps the other families will be cooperative."

"Each family put forward a champion," I growled. "Would you feel so sanguine if you discovered a group of men fought for the right to fuck *Isa?*" I asked, referring to the girl who had captivated him.

He watched her, much like I'd taken to watching Thalia after arriving back in the States a few months prior. The only difference was that he had the ability to manipulate and control her life.

I could not.

He glared at me with a snarl twisting his mouth, his eyes filled with loathing that promised to strangle me in my sleep. I still needed to get used to that coming from the man who cared about no one.

"We'll take the city immediately," I growled.

"The wedding is not for two months. We need time to recoup our losses before we launch a full attack on Philadelphia. The wise move is to wait and to plan. The grander the statement we make with our first assault, the more we can minimize the consequences later on. I understand your anger, Calix, but Damianos will not touch her until their wedding night," Rafe said, standing from the stool at the island and turning to face me fully. "You have waited twelve years for this moment. Do not fuck it up by acting impulsively now."

"Fine," I growled, turning and making my way for the bedroom I'd called home since we came to Chicago to help Matteo Bellandi with his war. I drew in a deep breath, trying to quell my rising dread. The Thalia I knew would not go quietly into a marriage she didn't want. The Thalia I knew fought and maneuvered, even as a young girl. She'd been far too smart for her own good, with a quiet rebelliousness hidden from all those who wanted to contain her.

As a child, she'd been obsessed with mythology and folklore. She'd been drawn to the beautiful creatures who hid monsters within, waiting for the right moment to devour their prey. From the ashes of those interests, she'd grown into a woman who belonged in the stories she loved so much. A beauty who smiled, giving the illusion of the perfect doll they expected her to be. But when the doors closed and the prying eyes disappeared, she morphed into the brutal woman who would cut down her enemies at the first opportunity.

The woman who held her hate within her heart, who embraced loneliness as her companion and readied herself to slaughter all who wronged her. Only the love for her sister kept her from acting on her violence, from utilizing the skills she learned in the quiet of the night alongside the man I'd planted in her security.

The ally I'd given her when I couldn't, who would protect her if things ever escalated past what Thalia was strong enough to handle on her own.

She'd been a girl who needed my protection. As a woman, she needed my acceptance and my love, and with it the ability to be the woman she was born to be. If I survived our wedding night, she would thrive at my side—a goddess born in the light who I would drag down to the pits of hell to make her mine.

I pushed open the door, stepping inside my bedroom and glancing to the wall of monitors where I watched Thalia move around her father's house. She stepped out of his office, her face twisted into a grimace as she withheld the grief of whatever her father had said to her. In the months since I'd started watching Thalia, I'd come to realize there was only one topic that could penetrate that shield she kept locked tightly around herself.

*Her mother.*

While Thalia and her mother hadn't been particularly close, as dictated by her father, Neri'd been the only thing she'd had that even remotely resembled family. The closest thing she'd known to love.

She made it to her room safely, leaning her back against the door as her lungs heaved with deep gasps of breath. Her fists clenched with the need to kill, to hurt and maim as they'd done to her. As she stepped away from the surface, she stretched her hands up to reach for the zipper at her back. Shoving the dress down her body frantically, she stripped away the layers of who they wanted her to be.

Her face transformed from that pleasant expression, hatred filling it as her amber eyes hardened into a glare she thought no one could see. My eyes moved over her body as she stepped through her room in pink undergarments. There wasn't an ounce of fat on her frame, her ribs protruding slightly from her form past what could be considered natural or healthy.

The strict diet her stepmother kept her on showed in every sharp edge of her body, on the exposed hip bones that drew attention down to her panty line. She stripped off her bra and underwear, grabbing a nightgown from her dresser and tugging it over her head frantically before she moved to the bathroom to wash the makeup from her face and brush her teeth.

Watching her go through her nighttime routine, I stripped off my clothes and settled into my bed with the laptop off my desk, resting it on one of the pillows as I got comfortable. I grabbed the e-reader off my nightstand, opening the fantasy romance Thalia had been reading earlier in the day.

She did exactly as I knew she would when she returned to her bedroom, grabbing her own device and opening the protective case she kept it in. She got comfortable on top of the covers, her eyes moving as she lost herself in the world of fantasy. I alternated between reading the pages of the book and watching her, studying her face and her body as she read.

I loved every twitch of her face. I lived for every intake of breath.

I lusted for the moments when her legs rubbed together to stall the ache building in her when she approached a sex scene, watched her cheeks tinge with hesitant desire that she didn't fully understand when she thought about a man taking her body.

As a woman who knew what it was to be treated like property, to be owned and have no free will of her own, I'd been shocked to discover that Thalia's choice of reading involved dominant men.

But they were dominant men who loved hard, who worshiped their women even as they controlled them.

As it always happened, her hand drifted down to the space between her legs as she read, biting her lip shyly as if someone could see her being naughty.

She didn't know how right she was.

I slid my hand down to grip my cock, pumping slowly as her long, delicate fingers slid down to touch her clit. Her hips rocked as if overcome with the need that one touch filled her with, the desperation for the freedom to touch and be touched written in every line of her body.

The light moan came through the computer speakers as I pumped, watching as she bit her lip to keep silent.

There had been a time when I hadn't been able to imagine wanting Thalia, when we'd been children too far apart in age for our relationship to be anything other than platonic. That had changed the moment I'd seen her as an adult after sending Christian to keep an eye on her and give me video access to the house. The moment I saw her, the pieces had clicked into place.

She'd become mine in the way a wife became her husband's.

And that was what I would be to her. Not solely a protector, but a husband in truth.

Her fingers danced over her flesh as she turned to her back, giving me an unobstructed view of the space between her thighs and the way she touched herself. I'd show her true passion soon enough, but until then I'd tolerate reading books and touching myself while I watched her.

The sight of her back arching off the bed and the soft swell of her breasts thrusting into the air sent me over the edge, pumping my cock furiously until I covered my stomach in my release.

As my heart raced and I watched Thalia come down from her high, impatience rose in me. She rolled to her stomach, revealing a fresh welt across her shoulders from her stepmother's favorite cane.

I didn't usually believe in killing women, but that bitch would die alongside her husband soon enough for what they'd done to my woman.

# 10

## THALIA

My hands remained clasped in front of me, carefully contained and controlled as I made my way down the steps. Lydia's plan for a grand entrance remained firmly in place, all of them watching me as I descended slowly in my heels. The light dress hung off my shoulders, lace covering my stomach and the tops of my thighs.

I ignored the weight of my father's stare and of all the ways he would judge me and find me lacking. Keeping my gaze intent on the man who stood beside him, I forced my face to remain impassive but pleasant. If he was to be my future, then pleasing my father was no longer my main concern.

Keeping Damianos happy would be my only purpose.

He stepped forward to meet me where the stairs curved around the corner at the bottom, holding out a hand for me to place mine in. Tipping his upper body forward, he touched his lips to the back of my knuckles. The split on his bottom lip scratched against my skin, a reminder of the violence from his fight only a few days prior.

Where he'd won me without a hint of concern for what I might think of it.

I shoved down the thought, tipping my lips into a slight smile as he stood straight. "You're as beautiful as ever, *η νύφη μου*," he said. I winced, only reminded of the contract that bound us together without any of the love that came with marriage in my favorite books.

It certainly didn't help that the overly affectionate name in Greek reminded me that there had been rumors of his rivalry with Calix. That the two boys had been competitors before Calix was banished, but I couldn't allow myself to care. Calix was forever gone from my life, and I had to do what was necessary to find peace with the life I had.

The very one he'd promised to protect me from.

"You're too kind," I said, my cheeks heating with the lie.

"I expect her home immediately after lunch," my father barked as Damianos offered his arm. I took it, wincing slightly when his body brushed against the side of mine. I'd been so trained to expect pain with human touch that I couldn't help the reaction when presented with a new, unknown person.

I wondered if it mattered to him to see the marks on my body. To see the welt across my shoulders that Lydia hadn't bothered to try to hide with a more modest dress. Instead, only the curtain of my dark hair offered any cover.

"Of course," Damianos said, grinning at my father's attempt to control the man who had recently taken over as the head of the Hasapis family. His father's battle against the cancer that riddled his body in the last year had made the transition of power necessary, and with it came the knowledge that Damianos was not a man content to remain one of several in power.

He'd start a war if the other families didn't keep him in

check, and I'd somehow had the misfortune to find myself the glue between the two factions. The last time such an alliance had been struck, it had ended with my mother dead.

I had to hope I wouldn't follow in her footsteps.

He guided me out the front doors, not pausing when I turned my face up to feel the sun on my skin. My seclusion had worsened after my mother's death, the result of private tutors who did their best to keep me trapped inside for all the daylight hours. Without my mother's attention, my father had allowed her field of narcissus flowers to wither and die in the yard, and I couldn't bring myself to step outside there in the rare moments I snuck away.

To feel the death of everything I loved so poignantly. That garden had been where I'd felt closest to my mother. It was where I'd met Calix.

So it seemed fitting in a way that it too would be dead.

His car waited, and I regretfully let him fold me into the passenger seat. His eyes fixated on the expanse of thigh as my dress rode up, making me swallow back the bile that came at the thought of his hands on me. I clenched my eyes closed as he shut the door and walked around to the other side.

Damianos wasn't an unattractive man. While his dark hair might have been longer than I suspected was my personal preference, he had a ruggedly handsome quality to his face, and broad shoulders as if he was truly a gladiator and didn't just engage in battle because of some ridiculous competitiveness.

We remained silent as he started the engine of his Porsche, pulling away from the entry to the house to turn down the long driveway. I wrung my hands in my lap, shoving down the feeling of horror that started to rise inside me. In my brief interactions with the other girls my age, I knew Damianos was considered a great catch.

That several wanted nothing more than to be contracted as his wife, given that there were no rumors of cruelty toward the women he slept with or the escorts the families employed. Still, the knowledge that he would touch me in less than two months' time made something insidious slither over my skin.

"Do you—" I paused to swallow down my nerves before starting over. "Is there anything you wish to know about me?" Perhaps if I could find a way to believe this was anything more than a business arrangement, then I would be able to find him more tolerable.

He glanced at me out of the corner of his eye as he drove through the main streets and toward the restaurant that wasn't far. "Like what?"

I bit my lip to fight the surge of anger that came as a response to his blatant dismissal of everything that was *me.* It was the only confirmation I needed that he was just like all the rest. That I would be his breeder, his trophy, tucked away and all but forgotten until he had the desire to use my body for his own pleasure.

I twisted to look out the window, tugging my dress down to the best of my ability as I felt suddenly exposed in a way I hadn't even moments before.

"Your father mentioned you liked history," he observed, as if the fact that he knew one small fact about me would ease whatever hurt he'd caused. He just didn't understand that he wasn't capable of hurting me. Not in that way. "He says you spend your free time buried in a book."

"Yes," I said, not bothering to admit that more often than not I read romance or fantasy books. "Ancient history specifically. Mythology. That sort of thing." The fact that he only knew my more tolerable hobby was salt in the wound.

My father wouldn't advertise the parts of me that he saw as a crack in the glass, a flaw to the pristine image he hoped to create in me.

"I enjoy artwork as well. Sketching, mostly," I said, watching as he clenched his jaw.

"But you have such lovely, soft hands." He reached across, taking mine in his grip and running his thumb over the smooth skin and eventually to the scars on my knuckles. "Wouldn't such a thing ruin them?"

I forced my best impression of the sultry smile Lydia had taught me to my face, raising my right hand to run over the back of his where he held mine. Turning it over, I separated our hands and ran delicate fingers over the rough skin on his palm. "You have calluses, but you are far from ruined," I murmured softly, watching as his hand twitched in my grip.

Turning my eyes up to look at him through my lashes, I watched as his eyes slid to mine. They darkened, as if I'd made a mistake and awoken something I couldn't have predicted would come so quickly. "I would much rather your nails dig into my shoulders than your calloused fingers," he said, deftly bringing us back to the reality that I was nothing but an inexperienced virgin who had no place playing games with a man.

I swallowed as my cheeks heated, moving to withdraw my hand. He clutched it in his as his attention refocused on the road. Resting the back of my hand against the top of his thigh, he seemed oblivious to my discomfort. "I think we should come to understand one another sooner to prevent misunderstandings later on."

"Okay," I whispered, tugging back on my hand.

"I'm not a man to toy with. I will not fall for manipulations through sex and teasing as your stepmother likely tried to teach you. Such things are done to catch a man, but you already caught me, sweetheart. We have no need for games between us, because in just a few weeks I'll spend my nights inside you." His voice was cold and impassive as he said the words, but there was no cruelty or taunting to them. Just a bleak picture of my reality.

He deftly pulled the Porsche into the parking lot, pulling up to the valet. "I understand," I whispered.

He made no move to get out, only releasing my hand and shifting in his seat to touch a hand to my bare upper back. His fingers skimmed the bruised welt from Lydia, gently prodding the skin. "But *this* is unacceptable. You will not suffer at my hands in this way," he said, pulling his hand away finally.

"I won't?"

"No, *η νύφη μου*. I will not harm you, and in return you will do what I expect of you as my wife," he said. "Can you do that for me?" I nodded slightly, holding still as he raised a hand to cup my cheek. Even if my instinct was to back away, to avoid the touch at all costs, I let his thumb trace over my cheekbone.

He shoved open the car door suddenly, walking around and pulling me out to take me inside so that we could have lunch together. The fortunate reality was that after we were married, he'd likely spend very little time with me.

My days would be my own. Even if my nights belonged to him.

# 11

## THALIA

*One week later.*

Christian lurked in the corner behind my mother's gardening shed, the same place he always hid when he needed a cigarette break. We'd never discussed why he helped me, or what his motivation was in risking my father's wrath to give me the outlet he did.

Slipping my shoes off, I crept around the corner behind him. Keeping my body as still as possible outside of my toes that dug into the ground with every step, I restrained the breath in my lungs.

Crouching low quickly, I swept a leg at his feet, groaning my frustration when the bastard hopped over it. "What the fuck!" I exclaimed with a laugh, jolting to my feet as he turned smiling eyes my way.

"You still breathe too heavy," he chuckled. I pursed my lips at him in a pout, straightening my dress as he put out his cigarette against the edge of the gardening shed and tucked it away in the vase he kept tucked beneath the shrubbery. "What do you want, Monster?" he asked with a sigh.

"I need a favor," I said, holding my head high as I

prepared to ask for the one thing I thought even Christian wouldn't give me. If anyone ever discovered the truth, which seemed like it would take careful planning on my part to avoid, he would be punished right alongside me. He'd pay the consequences with his life.

Guilt consumed me at the thought, making me hesitate to voice the favor. It'd be stupid and selfish and *pointless* in the end.

"What is it?" he asked, his brow furrowing in concern.

"Nothing," I said with a smile.

"Thalia," he said, reaching out a hand very slowly to take mine in his. "You know you can ask me for anything. If it's within my ability, I'll give it to you."

"I wanted a night. To be free to choose who I want for my first time," I said with a swallow. "If there's a way to do it without getting caught, then I have to try. But I need to find a way to do that without involving you. I won't let anyone else suffer for my choices."

He leaned back into the shed, crossing his arms over his chest and staring at me with wide eyes. "You want me to help you get laid?" He swallowed as if the thought was insufferable, and I pushed down the old hurts of being an awkward girl who nobody ever looked at twice.

"No. I want to choose for myself, and I think I can manage to convince one man to fuck me." I laughed. "I just need the window for it to be possible."

He sighed, running his hand over his face. "Okay. Give me a week or two to figure something out and make the arrangements. I can't guarantee anything, but I'll see what I can do," he said, nodding back toward the house where Lydia poked her head out to look for me. "You get your ass back to the house and act like you didn't just ask me to help you commit suicide. Fuck," he groaned.

I flung my arms around him for a brief hug before making my way back to the house, keeping with the shadows until I could come up into the still living gardens at the side of the manor itself and pretend I'd been sitting among the flowers.

Nobody could know.

# 12

## CALIX

My cell vibrated on the desk as I looked over the reports Enzo had sent to the house. The Bellandis wouldn't leave me to fight my war alone, not after Rafael and I had given everything to help them in theirs.

By the time Thalia's wedding came, we'd be ready. We just needed to develop the perfect strategy in the meantime. I picked up the phone when Christian's name flashed on the screen, knowing that he would be safely tucked away in his tiny apartment at the late hour. "What's wrong?" I asked, jolting to my feet as every muscle in my body tensed. The thought of Thalia being harmed at all was enough to send me into a furious rage, but for her to be hurt severely enough that he would risk his cover to contact me?

It was unthinkable.

"She's fine," he reassured me quickly. "I promise. No one has hurt her in the last few days from what I've seen."

"Then what the fuck do you want?" I snarled, dropping my weight back into my chair.

"She came to me with a request today. It isn't something that I'm comfortable dealing with on my own, so you might have to move up your timetable." He gave an uncomfortable chuckle, and I could just imagine the man rubbing the back of his neck with his other hand.

"What are you talking about?" I asked, exhaustion creeping into my tone. Every waking hour had been spent making arrangements and contacting allies in the region who would be willing to go up against the five remaining families to have me reinstated.

Or to kill them all and take the city for myself. Either option worked just as well for me.

"She doesn't want to lose her virginity to Damianos," he said suddenly. "She asked me to help her get a window where she can find a man and..." he trailed off, the hesitance in his voice making me grind my teeth together.

"Don't you fucking say it," I warned with a growl.

He ignored me, continuing on. "She wants to find someone to fuck her, so she can say that for just once she had a choice in who she took to bed. I'm going to go out on a limb and say that you are *not* down with that idea, so how would you like me to handle it? I saw the look on her face, man. If I say no, she'll just find another way."

My chest vibrated with the need to rip his vocal chords out of his throat for planting the image of Thalia with someone else in my head, but as much as I hated his insistence on telling me what I didn't want to hear, I knew he was right.

She was nothing if not rebellious at her core. She was never going to go quietly into a loveless marriage.

"Set it up. Get me a day and a time, and I'll fucking be there," I said, gripping the edge of the desk with my free hand.

"You're going to stop her?" Christian asked, his voice full

of questions. We both knew Thalia knowing I'd returned would ruin all our careful planning.

"No. I'm not," I snapped, pulling the phone away from my ear and jabbing the screen with furious fingers. I stood from the desk and made my way to the screens to watch Thalia sleeping peacefully in her bed.

She was beautiful, peaceful, as she laid there curled up into a ball beneath her blanket. Like an angel of death, just waiting for me to defile her.

If she was so desperate to be ruined, I'd happily oblige.

# 13

## THALIA

*Two weeks later.*

I paced back and forth in my room in the ballet flats I'd slipped onto my feet. I didn't own anything even remotely resembling sneakers, at my father and stepmother's insistence.

With my shoes for the night packed into the designer tote slung under my arm, my lungs heaved with the panic that threatened to take everything from me. By the end of the night, I wouldn't be a virgin.

By the end of the night, I'd have experienced what it was to be normal for just a few hours. To do something foolish and impulsive purely for the sake of it, because *I wanted to.*

Glancing at the watch on my wrist, I blew out a breath as the time finally reflected ten at night. The quiet knock on my door came promptly, leaving me to move toward it as quietly as I could and pull the door open slowly. Christian's kind face stared back at me on the other side, and he waved a hand to signal me to step out. "You've got everything?" he asked, looking down my body with a furrow to his brow. "Where did you get that dress?"

"Lydia has been filling my closet with clothes more appropriate for pleasing my husband," I whispered. "Is there something wrong with it?" The dark and fitted dress hugged what I had for curves, extending down past my knees except for the slit up the thigh.

He rolled his eyes to the ceiling, muttering to himself before grimacing and shaking his head. "Nope. Great, let's go," he said, turning to stroll down the hallway for the stairs.

"Wait, we're just going to walk out the front door?" I asked.

"Yes, hurry up or we'll miss our window," he grunted, taking my hand in his and hurrying me down the stairs. One of my father's security stood there, facing the wall on the opposite side and diligently pretending he didn't see us as we pulled the doors open and stepped outside.

"What about my father?" I asked.

"Gone to the stables for the night. They brought in a couple girls from New York, so he'll be occupied until morning," Christian said as he shoved me into the backseat of the waiting car. He climbed in beside me, tapping the back of the headrest and signaling the driver to make his way down the driveway as I fought back the surge of sickness at the thought of my father being occupied with the escorts.

"What about Lydia?" I asked. "If she wakes up and notices I'm gone, this will all be for nothing."

"Sleeping pill in her wine. No one will notice you're gone as long as you get back before morning. We should be safely back on the property by 4 a.m. Understood?" he asked, nodding to my watch. "Can you set an alarm on that thing?"

I took my phone from my bag, setting an alarm for three in the morning just to be safe as the driver made his way down the road. Without a single glance toward the backseat, he seemed determined to pretend he hadn't seen me. As if I wasn't in his car, and he wasn't defying my father's very strict orders that I be kept at the house with very few exceptions.

Namely, when he or my step-mother accompanied me to required outings.

We pulled up to a hotel in the center of the city, and I changed out my flats for heels quickly before allowing Christian to pull me from the car. "Aren't we too close?"

"We can't go too far if we want to get you home in time. Nobody will recognize you here. I've cleared the guest list, and aside from you only hotel patrons will be allowed tonight. It may limit your..." He swallowed down his distaste, finishing with, "options, but it will keep you alive."

I nodded, biting my lip hesitantly before lunging at him for a quick hug. "Thank you," I mumbled.

"Don't thank me just yet," he said, his voice catching with emotion. "Just be safe, yeah?"

"Of course," I said, watching as he got back into the car and waited. Turning and striding into the hotel, I made my way to the elevators to go to the rooftop bar. With my heart in my throat, I almost couldn't hear the dull thrum of the elevator music. The numbers on the panel rose one by one, lighting up as if counting down my last chance to change my mind.

There would be no backing out for me, not if I wanted to be able to look myself in the mirror come morning.

Having an adventure meant taking risks. I would just have to do whatever it took to make sure that I was the only one who paid the price for what I would do.

As the elevator doors opened, the steady thrum of jazz filled the night air. Stars twinkled vaguely overhead, drowned out even on the rooftop by the light pollution of the city. Deciding to make my way to the center of the space,

I headed straight for the bar with my nerves threatening to tear me in two. The bartender's eyes met mine briefly as I approached, and she smirked once before she went back to her work and poured white wine.

I sat on a stool, curling my hand around the glass of wine that landed in front of me. "I didn't order this," I said, pushing it back toward her with a shy smile.

"It's on the house, honey. I know when a woman just needs a fucking drink every now and then," she said.

"Is it that obvious?" I asked, raising the glass to my lips and taking a sip. The bitterness of the liquid caught me by surprise, coating my tongue in a dry flavor that wasn't entirely pleasant.

"Not a fan of wine?" she asked with a chuckle, and I shook my head shyly.

"Not a drinker of anything, to be honest," I said, forcing down another sip. I knew people swore by the way alcohol made them relax, and if anyone needed that tonight? It was me. I was about to lose my virginity to a stranger and risk certain death if I was caught.

"You should be careful of your surroundings if you aren't used to drinking, Little One," a male voice said behind me. I spun in the stool, the name that poured off his lips nearly making me stumble to the floor with the suddenness of the movement. My eyes landed on his the moment he reached out his hands to catch me around the waist, stabilizing me so I didn't tumble to the floor. His hands seared me through the fabric of my dress, an inescapable heat that seemed to sink beneath the surface of my flesh and dig straight into the core of who I was.

"Sorry," I mumbled, sliding my ass further onto the stool. His hands never left my waist, one of his thighs tucked between my knees ever so slightly. Still his gaze stayed focused on mine. Not on the heaving of my breasts as they shoved higher with each lungful of air I sucked back in my nervousness.

"Exactly how much have you had to drink?" he asked, his lips cocking to the side with the barest hint of a smile. Those stunning metallic eyes shone down at me, making my heart race in my chest. While I had no doubt that they were blue or some other enviable color, I couldn't help but be reminded of the silver of Calix's eyes.

Of his boyishly handsome face as he made me believe that someone in the world cared about me.

"It wasn't that," I admitted with a flush as I tore my eyes from his. My hand slid down the fabric of his suit jacket, clasping his forearm in my grip. I started to grip him so that I could push away his touch, but stopped at the last moment with a twist of my lips. "Nobody has called me Little One in a very long time. You surprised me, is all."

"Hmm," he hummed thoughtfully, grasping the stool next to me in one of his hands. He tugged it closer, settling on the seat and enclosing my legs inside his until I felt trapped. But the movement didn't fill me with fear as I might have expected, only serving to give me the sense that he would protect me from whatever dangers might be lurking around the room.

I took another sip of wine to steady myself, wondering how on earth women understood the rules of picking up a man. He might have been interested, but he also could have merely acted out of interest in being gentlemanly and keeping me from making a foolish mistake.

Perhaps he simply saw through the bravado I'd tried to don the moment I walked into the bar.

"So not Little One, then," he murmured, and something inside my chest eased. I wouldn't have been able to go to bed with a man who called me the same pet name as Calix. It would have felt like a betrayal to all that he'd meant to me once upon a time. "So what should I call you?"

I wrinkled my nose, running my finger over the base of my wine glass to calm the fidgeting that wanted to make me squirm in my seat. "Nothing," I said softly. "No names."

He raised his brows at me, huffing out a light, shocked laugh. He paused for a moment, studying my face as he tried to understand my motivation. I knew it must have seemed ridiculous not to give someone even my first name, but I needed to stay detached.

One night of sex. One time to feel like maybe I was using the man just as much as he used me.

"If I don't tell you my name, what will you scream when I make you come tonight?" he asked, his full lips tipping into an arrogant smirk that caught the breath in my lungs. I bit my lip, turning my face away as my cheeks heated. "That is what you're looking for, isn't it, my beauty?"

"I haven't even told you my name, and you already think to own me?" I said with more snap than intended. Doubt coursed through me, wondering if it was even possible to just have one pleasant experience. People did it all the time, so I had to believe there was someone in that bar who would be able to give me what I wanted.

He just might not be quite as breathtaking as the man in front of me, with his dark hair and sinfully light eyes shining down at me. "For tonight. I am not a man who plays games or beats around the bush when it comes to what I want," he said, leaning forward to rest his palm on the bare skin just above my knee.

"And what is it you want?" I asked, staring down at that hand.

"The same thing I expect brought you here, sitting in a

bar alone and swearing off names," he chuckled. Another man stepped up to us, opening his mouth to speak briefly before a single glare from my handsome stranger sent him scurrying away.

"That was hardly necessary," I said with a laugh.

"I don't share," he growled in warning.

I lifted his hand off my knee, standing in the small space between his legs and grabbing my wine glass. "Well, I suppose it is fortunate for me that you don't own me. I'll seek my entertainment elsewhere." Moving to step out from the trap of his spread legs, I winced when he didn't budge. Even with the crowd of people filling the rooftop and the bartender behind me watching us with rapt attention, dread filled me at the thought of having to deal with a forceful man.

I'd had enough of men who thought to take from me without giving a single thought to what I might want.

"Release me," I hissed, watching as his eyes lit in response to the challenge in my voice.

"If I were to do that, we would lose out on a very valuable opportunity that we are now presented with," he said, flashing me his perfect teeth in a broad grin. "You're angry with me. I would very much like to have all that fire wrapped around me while I fuck you, my beauty," he added, stretching out a hand to cup my cheek in his hand. I jerked back from the contact, glaring at him as his hand followed and settled against the side of my neck. His thumb stroked over the delicate chord of my throat, leaving me with a feeling of vulnerability that I was all too used to. But whereas when my father hurt me all I felt was pain and fear, the stranger's touch evoked something different altogether.

Heat bloomed between my thighs, my body warming in the way it did when I read romance novels in my bed at night. Biting my tongue to stifle my reaction and the moan that threatened to surface, I stared up at him in shock. I hadn't pictured a hate fuck for my first time, not being a virgin.

I'd imagined someone gentler, something sweeter. But there was no denying the reaction in my body and the appeal of his words. When I read, it wasn't the sweet love-making scenes that forced my hand between my legs to relieve the ache, but the rough and passionate ones that left me breathless.

His touch promised all the things I'd read about, the very desire I'd only ever dreamt of having. He was silent as he watched me process my choices, studying the features of my face as if he could see every thought as it floated through my mind. I should have said no.

I should have called Christian to take me home before I made a mistake that I could never undo.

"Do you have a room?" I asked instead, my pulse thumping against his thumb where he stroked over it with gentle pressure.

He nodded, his light eyes turning wolfish as he drew his hand away from my neck and tucked it around my waist. The moment I was pressed into his side, he strode toward the elevators, guiding me to the place where he'd take what I gave and seal my fate.

For better or worse.

# 14

## CALIX

My hand at her waist felt like it had always belonged there. Like the more than a decade of separation had changed both of us in synchronization somehow, and we'd grown into the perfect match for the people we'd grown to be as adults.

On the other side of our tragedy, she was mine and I was hers.

She just didn't know it yet.

Her silence grated at me, and I knew I needed to try to be mindful of her virginity. While I'd watched her fingers dance over her clit at night and slip inside her tight heat, she'd always been cautious. The knowledge that her betrothed would expect her to be a virgin and she'd been saving that for *him* only served to drive my need to claim her and make her mine higher. By the end of the night, I alone would know what she felt like on the inside.

As I shoved open the door to my suite, I tried to convince myself it didn't matter that she hadn't recognized me. That there was no shame in that, because she'd only been a girl when I'd left. Even if I'd have recognized her anywhere, life hadn't been kind to Thalia. I didn't know what it was like to go through life in shades of gray, but I imagined it made people less recognizable. All light eyes looked the same. All dark hair looked the same.

She stepped inside hesitantly, her back straighter than a rod and her head held high to look every bit the princess her father had tried to mold her into. But Thalia was never meant to be a princess or a queen, she'd been born to be a warrior.

To bathe in the blood of our enemies.

It would take her some time to understand that they were one and the same, but the time would come when she would.

I closed the door behind me gently, moving into the suite to stand behind her. She stilled at the feeling of my chest against her back, her breath hitching in a way that I instinctively knew wasn't in desire. It would take time to get rid of those impulses, of her instinctual expectation of pain.

Gathering her dark curtain of hair in my grip, I pulled it over one shoulder and revealed her smooth olive skin to my gaze. There wasn't a blemish marking the top of her shoulder, only the faint remainder of a welt across her shoulder blades that made me grit my teeth. She moved as if she might step away, freezing when I gripped her hair tighter and pulled her head to the side. Careful not to pull, only to put her where I wanted her, I moved slowly until my lips touched her skin.

A gasp escaped her, making me wish I'd positioned her in a way that I could see her face. Instead I trailed my lips over the delicate flesh, touching gentle kisses and working to start preparing her to take what I would give her.

She allowed it for a few moments, her slim body writhing against me as desire built in her. "I thought you were going to fuck me," she murmured softly, a teasing challenge to the words that made me smile against her skin. Spreading my mouth open, I sank my teeth into her shoulder to suppress the fight.

She moaned, her voice breathy as I released her and spun her to face me. With a hand still buried in her hair, I tilted her head back until she had no choice but to look up at me. With her pouty lips parted slightly, the desire to taste her came over me. Leaning forward slowly, I brushed my lips against hers. She held my stare, and I willed her to feel me.

*To see me.*

Her hands came up to rest against my chest as I pulled away, touching my forehead to hers and wondering what it would take for her to see me as I was. For who I was. Would she remain oblivious until the moment I revealed myself? The thought bothered me more than it should.

I leaned forward, touching my lips to hers again and tracing the parted seam of her lips with my tongue. She moaned for me, opening wider as I slid inside and claimed her mouth as mine. The first part of her to be possessed by me, the first part of her that I would take. As she adjusted to the softness of my kiss and the slow and erotic tangle of our mouths, I exerted more pressure.

Her eyes drifted closed finally as I plundered her mouth. She inhaled suddenly as I released her hair, dragging a hand down over her arm to grab the zipper at the back of her dress. Pulling it down slowly, I waited for the moment when she'd come to her senses and realize the dangers of being so reckless.

For the moment when she'd walk away, not knowing that what would happen between us was inevitable. Whether it happened here and now or on our wedding night was her choice, but in the end Thalia would be mine and mine alone.

Instead, she pulled her lips away from mine and brushed the straps of her dress off her shoulders. The forest green fabric dropped to her waist, bunching around her hips until she slid her hands down to it and shimmied out of it. She stood nearly naked in front of me with a tease in her eyes as she backed away a step, unconcerned with the fact that it was the first time she'd been nude with a man. Only a scrap of lace covering her pussy hid her from my view, her small breasts high and perky on her frame without a bra.

The heels on her feet made her legs look even longer, and she bit her lip as a trace of insecurity filled her face when I didn't move. Wrongly assuming I may not want her, when the reality was that I couldn't move or take my eyes off her.

Finally shrugging my jacket off my shoulders, I tossed it over the back of the arm chair at the side of the room. Thalia's eyes narrowed in on my fingers as I worked open the buttons of my shirt one by one. I smirked at her when her eyes heated, throwing my shirt to join the jacket and then stripping off my shoes and pants. "Last chance, my beauty," I murmured. Every second where the words sat between us made my deception worse. Every time I used the name that didn't belong to her, it struck against the deepest part of me. We were finally reunited, but still so far away.

I left my boxer briefs on for the moment, closing the distance between us again. She tilted her head up to accept the kiss I didn't give her, taking her waist in my hands instead and tossing her onto the bed behind her. She giggled lightly as she bounced against the surface, the sound trailing off as I climbed up and spread her legs to slip my hips between them.

My cock nestled against her pussy, her heat like a brand through the only clothing remaining. With the warmth in her amber eyes, I leaned my weight over hers. Pebbled nipples rubbed against my chest, driving me mad with the need to drive inside her.

I kissed her, groaning when her cautious hand slid between us to touch my cock. She nipped my bottom lip before pulling away. "If I wanted gentle, I could have picked a dozen other men," she said. A warning grumbled in my chest; the very idea of her choosing anyone but me would have been disastrous for all involved.

I'd kill anyone who dared to touch her.

"Fuck me," she ordered.

"I'll hurt you," I returned, raising an eyebrow at her. I couldn't say any more than that, because the knowledge that she was a virgin wasn't something a stranger could have. As much as I'd wanted Thalia to recognize me, it was truly for the best that she hadn't.

She nodded. "I want it to hurt," she said, a questioning hurt filling her gaze. She couldn't understand that there was nothing wrong with having desires like that, and she'd never be able to fulfill them in a safe way with a husband she couldn't trust, but everything about our first time would be wrong if I gave her what she asked for.

She deserved so much more than to be brutally fucked by a stranger in a hotel, and everything inside me rebelled against what had become of her, that this was how desperate she was for even the ability to make her own choice just *once.* It seemed like such a simple thing to anyone else. Her right as a human being.

But for her it was an act of rebellion at best. Suicide at worst, because if her father found out what she did, if Damianos rejected her if he realized the truth?

Origen would have no use for her.

It was very fortunate for my Little One that she would never marry Damianos.

I leaned forward, nipping her bottom lip with my teeth before surging inside her mouth. I kissed her like I wanted to consume her, painting every corner of her with my possession. With only our undergarments between us, she squirmed beneath me. Rolling her hips against the outline of my cock, she gasped into my mouth at the pressure it put on her clit. I was overwhelmed with the need to feel her slick heat rubbing against me, to glide through her parted lips and drive her mad with the teasing thrusts long before I ever slid inside her. But Thalia would need to know who was in charge, and her very demand for me to fuck her before I was ready went against everything I knew about myself.

As my wife, she'd need to know exactly what to expect from me, and there was no time like the present to start with her education.

I grabbed her hands away from my body, pinning them to the bed beside her hips as she narrowed her gaze up at me. "I think you've misread the situation," I purred, gliding my lips away from her mouth and toward the sensitive skin of her neck. I trailed them over her skin, feeling her squirm and press up against me as her body was lost to the instinct that lurked inside her. "You are not in charge of anything when you're in my bed, my beauty."

"Unless you live in a hotel, I'm not sure how that's relevant," she said quickly. The comeback came with such ease that I chuckled hoarsely. While it hadn't been anything dramatic, the very fact that she had one after being so beaten down by the life I couldn't protect her from proved everything I'd always known about her.

She was stronger than anyone imagined.

"If you're in it, it's my bed," I murmured, biting her ear briefly before gliding down over her collarbone to touch my lips to the swell of her breast. She shuddered beneath me, her body going taut as she prepared for the contact she'd so desperately craved. With my hands occupied to pin her down, all I had to work with was my mouth.

But it was enough.

"I think your logic is faulty," she gasped as I sank my teeth into her flesh, biting harder than I should in my desperation to mark her. "Don't," she warned, seeming to realize the dangers of returning home to her stepmother with bruises. It took everything in me to pull back and run my tongue over the mark gently.

Releasing one of her wrists, I gripped her breast in my palm as my mouth found her other nipple. Her back arched off the bed as her free hand plunged into my hair. Grasping and pulling at the short strands, she kept me pressed tightly to her as I worshiped her and every inch of her torso with my mouth. By the time I'd slid down between her legs, she quivered beneath me with desperation. Her amber eyes met mine as I tugged her underwear down her thighs and tossed them to the side once they were freed.

She spread her legs wider for me without needing me to ask, her body bared to me without a hint of hesitation. She didn't need to care what I thought of her when she thought she would never see me again, and she most definitely didn't want to waste the opportunity to feel what she probably never would again.

Men like Damianos had no need to make sure their wives enjoyed their sex life. Not when they were already paid for and unable to escape.

Pinning her arms to her sides once more, I moved into

her slowly. Holding her eyes as I ran my tongue from her entrance to her clit in a slow glide. She moaned, shoving her hips up at me more firmly in an attempt to get more pressure as I kept the touch of my mouth against her soft. "What do you want, my beauty?" I murmured.

"More."

"Manners," I reprimanded her, gently biting into the soft flesh of her thigh.

"Please," she groaned. Smirking into her flesh, I dove forward and gave her everything she wanted. I devoured her with intense sweeps of my tongue, shoving it inside her and fucking her with it while she gasped and moaned. "Fucking *please*," she begged again, squirming until my mouth returned to her clit. I wrapped my lips around it, sucking it lightly and working it with my tongue until she shattered beneath me. Her eyes clamped shut, separating me from her in those intense moments of her orgasm. I determined in that moment that her next one would be with her eyes on mine. That I'd watch as the pleasure consumed her.

When her breathing relaxed and she opened those stunning eyes, I released her hands and crawled off the bed. I wanted nothing more than to pretend the condom waiting in my pants pocket didn't exist, so desperate to feel her pussy wrapped around me with nothing between us. But a one-night stand would wear a condom, and I wanted there to be no doubt that our child was conceived when she was already my wife.

Tearing the packet open with my teeth, I watched the first moments of caution settle over Thalia's features and the face that I'd come to recognize as well as my own in the time since I'd started watching her obsessively. "Last chance," I said, a challenge in my tone.

Daring her to back down was the fastest way to ensure

she followed through, because there was no possibility of her leaving my bed as a virgin. Not after what we'd started.

She raised her chin, watching as I shoved my boxer briefs down and rolled the condom onto my cock. Her lips parted in shock for a moment, the reality of what was about to be inside her giving her another moment of pause.

Prowling onto the bed between her legs, I settled over her and spread her wide. With the wet heat of her pussy searing me even through the condom, I slid through her oversensitive flesh as I watched her face. The smart thing would be for her to give the stranger a warning. To tell him that he was about to fuck a virgin so he might have a chance to be more gentle with her.

But even as I gave Thalia the opportunity to be honest with me, she kept her lips firmly clamped around her secret.

With a ragged groan, I notched myself at her entrance and watched her face. Even though I wanted to have my lips on hers when I first slid inside her, I forced myself to keep separated. To watch her face and give her the chance to tell me if it was too much or too fast.

I drove inside, shoving through her tender tissue more harshly than I should, given what I knew. Even with the force of it, I couldn't get far. Not with the way she was choking the life out of my cock. She groaned, bending her neck so that she curled in on herself as a startled scream caught in her throat. "Something you need to tell me, Beauty?" I asked, pulling back and then pressing forward firmly again. "Because this feels like something I should know."

"Fuck you," she hissed, baring her teeth at me as she reached down to grab my ass in her hands. She pulled me closer, impaling herself on my cock as I pressed through that barrier inside her. She yelped, leaning up to press her mouth to my shoulder. Teeth sinking into my flesh, she marked me in the way I wanted to mark her.

When she finally settled back onto the bed, I moved inside her with slow but firm thrusts. Taking her in the way I wanted and touching my lips to hers. Our breath mingled as she wrapped her legs around my waist.

Slowly the pinch of pain on her face faded to something else entirely, shock flooding her features as she realized the depths of pleasure that could be found with me inside her. With one hand wrapped around to hold the back of her thigh, I slid the other beneath her neck and held her exactly where I wanted her. She took me deep, accepting the pounding pressure of me as her pussy spasmed beneath me with a coming orgasm.

I wanted it. Wanted to keep it for myself.

"Eyes on me," I ordered, touching my forehead to hers. The intimacy of the moment was something I'd never dreamed to have, because it wouldn't have made sense with anyone but Thalia. She'd always been meant to be mine.

Her breath caught in her throat as she came with nothing but the movement of my cock inside her, her amber eyes turning molten as her pussy choked the cum out of my cock and I followed her over the edge into a blinding release of my own and filled the condom.

She lay beneath me, panting for breath as I dreaded what came next.

Knowing she would walk away from me wouldn't stop the sting when she actually did it.

# 15

THALIA

The loss of him immediately settled over me as he pulled out. He left me in the bed to dispose of the condom, and that empty hollowness that had threatened since the moment my mother had died claimed me once more.

I'd been foolish to risk everything for one night with a stranger who didn't even know my name. I'd risked leaving Malva entirely vulnerable if anyone discovered what I'd done. Considering that I had to behave for the right to even spend time with my younger sister, my father wouldn't hesitate to remove me from her life entirely.

I'd be a bad influence on her, and in that moment, my father's voice that echoed in my head was right. I would never have allowed her to do something like this. Not knowing what the cost might be.

I sat on the edge of the bed, curling my fingers around the edge of the mattress as the soreness between my thighs throbbed with pain.

And for what?

Pushing to my feet, I grabbed my underwear off the floor

where he'd tossed them and tugged them up my thighs. I winced when the wet mess between my legs touched the fabric, but using the bathroom was the last thing on my mind.

I needed to get home before someone noticed I was gone.

"You wound me, trying to sneak off without even saying goodbye," the stranger said as he stepped out of the bathroom. He hadn't bothered to cover his manhood, leaving it to swing indecently between his legs. Even softening after his release, the length caught my eyes and I couldn't help but wonder exactly *how* that had fit inside me.

"My apologies, I know you care about my manners," I spat, turning to give him my back as I grabbed my dress off the floor.

The air around me went still as I stood straight, and I glanced over my shoulder to find him staring at the scars crisscrossing my back and the flesh of my ass intently. His nostrils were flared, his jaw clenched tightly.

I shut mine briefly, drawing in a deep breath as I realized my mistake. The light from the open bathroom door illuminated the faint light lines that had faded over the years. It had been a long time since I'd done something to earn a caning quite like those.

Raising my arms to pull my dress over my head, I winced as rough fingers ran along the thick scar on my lower back. "He will get what's coming to him," he said, leaning forward to touch his lips to the scar. My skin twitched beneath his mouth, the gentleness and care in the contact drawing a shiver from me.

I would never know such a sweet touch again.

"Who said it was a he?" I asked, trying to deflect from the well of emotion surging inside of me. My father wasn't the only abuser in that house of nightmares, and even though the worst of the blows had come from his steady and unrelenting hand, my stepmother had never been innocent.

Neither had many of the guards who'd watched my father abuse and humiliate me, getting off on the searing pain that split my skin in half.

The stranger took my dress in his hands, tossing it to the chair at the side of the room as he grasped my chin in his grip and turned me to face him. "You're beautiful, even more so now."

"Sounds like you have a kink for hurting women," I snarled, flinching back as his lips came closer to mine. The heat of his breath against my swollen flesh reminded me of all the savagery in his kiss when he'd taken me, bringing a flush of heat to my sore core that I wished I could deny.

Nothing about this conversation should have been a turn on. Talking about my caning with a stranger who would *never* be able to understand the misery of a life that wasn't my own should have cooled all the impulses that seemed to drive me toward him relentlessly.

I couldn't explain the connection or the feeling that I'd met him before. That I somehow knew him or that he meant the words when he said that the person who hurt me would get what was coming to him.

Those plush lips of his brushed against my cheek as his light eyes drifted closed. "I have a lot of kinks, but that is not one of them," he said with a smirk. "A mysterious, strong woman who bears the scars of her abuse without fear however..." he trailed off, slipping a hand around the front of my hip and between my thighs. His fingers slid inside my underwear and through the wet mess he'd left, a groan rattling in his chest when my hips moved of their own accord and my ass pressed into his hardening length. "That, my cock can't seem to get enough of."

He dipped a finger inside me, watching my face for the pain he must have known I felt. I didn't give him a reaction, keeping my face as stoic as possible. While I didn't think he would hurt me or use my pain against me, I needed the distance between us. My scars out in the open had left me vulnerable, knowing that I'd dreaded the moment the rejection came from *any* man who saw me without my clothes.

Who wanted to look at an ass covered in white lines?

"How sore are you?" he asked, walking forward and maneuvering my body so I had no choice but to move with him. The bed loomed closer as we moved and the breath caught in my lungs from the implication that I wouldn't be leaving the room just yet.

I still had time, but was I able to take him back inside me so soon? With all my old vulnerabilities in the open? The scars made me more *me*, not just a strange girl in the night who would be gone by morning.

My knees and thighs hit the edge of the mattress, and his hand touched the space between my shoulder blades. He pressed me forward, bringing panic to the surface as memories threatened to overwhelm me.

I whimpered, and his hand stilled so suddenly I knew he must have understood that it wasn't a whimper of anticipation. My heart thumped in my chest as my eyes clenched tight, trying to chase away the phantom hands of my stepmother tasked with putting me into position, with pinning my hands to the surface and reminding me that it was my own fault.

Trying to remind myself that the softness of the mattress was different than the cold wood of my father's desk.

"It's just me, my beauty. I will *never* hurt you," he

murmured, sweeping my hair off my neck. He paused, waiting for a moment to allow me to catch my breath and chase away the shadows of my nightmare. "You didn't answer me."

His voice took on a teasing lilt, pushing back the demons as that inexplicable urge to argue with him rose in me.

Not because he was wrong, but because I *could.*

He wouldn't cane me for talking back or tell me to remember my place; he'd take anything I said with a grin and enjoy the banter for what it was. I hummed, considering my answer as I tried to embrace my last moments of freedom before I went back to my gilded cage.

"I'm not sure you fucked me hard enough for that," I murmured. His deep chuckle vibrated the air behind my back, his hand returning to my shoulders and pressing me forward until I bent over the bed. When my nipples brushed against the bedding, they pebbled in response to the friction as his hand trailed down over my spine and made me arch my back.

His weight disappeared from behind me for a moment, and the crinkle of a foil packet sounded. When he returned, he peeled my panties off and let them bunch around my knees. The swollen head of his cock slid between my legs and rubbed against me as he groaned. "We'll have to fix that then," he said, not bothering to call me out on the lie. He trusted me to know my body better than he did, and even though he was a stranger that made something pang inside my chest.

A dull ache that reminded me of all I'd lost, and everything I would never have again.

He slid inside me, pounding deep enough on the first stroke that I cried out as the ache flared to life. "But I thought you weren't sore, Beauty?" he asked, gripping my hips in his hands and tugging me back further onto his cock. He brushed against the end of me, threatening to fuck through me if he got any deeper.

"I think you're terribly full of yourself," I said, my voice arching higher as he drew back and pounded inside me again.

"No, Little One," he said, his voice drifting lower as my heart seized in my chest. Even as a coincidence, the name was *wrong* to hear a man say as he moved inside me. A bastardization of everything Calix had meant to me.

But Calix was gone. He'd left me behind and moved on with his life without once trying to come back for me to save me from what he knew must have been a miserable existence. The man who slid his cock through my pussy was real, flesh and blood and warm.

Making me feel for the first time since I'd lost Calix and my mother to my father's vindictiveness.

"*You* are the one full of me," he growled, wrapping my hair up in his hand and pulling back. I rose up to my hands, moaning as his hips slapped against my ass and he set a punishing rhythm. He didn't seem concerned about the scars covering my skin or anything other than chasing his release inside me. The weighted stare of his eyes on those marks on my ass should have made me uncomfortable, instead it only drove me higher. Being seen for who and what I was and still found beautiful was heady. "Touch yourself," he ordered.

When I didn't move to do just that, he reached between the mattress and my body. Pulling me back from the edge of the bed just slightly, he slapped his fingers against my pussy just hard enough that I jolted in his grip. "What the hell?" I asked as he shoved deep and held still.

With his head pressed against the end of me firmly, the

pressure felt endless. "When I tell you to do something, you fucking do it," he growled. His hand left my pussy, gliding up to where I grasped the bedding firmly and positioning it between my legs. "You expect me to believe that these beautiful fingers don't dance over your pretty little pussy when you lie in bed at night?" he asked, guiding them into a slow roll over my clit as he drew his length out and then drove back in sharply. "You're going to need the pleasure when I'm done with you."

He abandoned my hand there, pausing for a moment to make sure that I did as he told me. His hand traveled up to my throat, grasping me around the front and pulling my back into his chest as he fucked me. My breathing restricted, my head going light until all that remained was the feel of him pounding up into me. His warm breath on my cheek as he panted and groaned his pleasure.

Still, my fingers circled my clit frantically, driving my pleasure higher to combat what would undoubtedly make me very sore come morning. "Fuck," I whispered as my vision blurred, the shadows of the room fading into bright white light that overtook my senses.

My ears rang with the force of my orgasm, only faintly aware of the driving thrusts of his cock still moving inside me and the brutal roar of his release as he pulled me down onto his cock and came.

When he released my throat, I fell forward. My body went limp and languid, and I cherished the moments where there was no consequence. Where there wasn't the threat of nightmares looming on the other side of sleep, and I could just curl into the bed he placed me in peacefully.

He left for a moment, returning quickly and curling himself around my body. "Sleep, Little One."

Sleep evaded me, knowing I needed to leave shortly

enough, but I allowed myself to enjoy the way his breathing evened out as he found his own rest.

It was only after he'd fallen asleep that panic seized my lungs and sent me hurrying from the bed as quietly as I could. My heart wanted to let him in, to accept him as someone I could care for when I could never.

But that wasn't what made panic seize my lungs.

He'd somehow known to guide my left hand between my legs.

# 16

## THALIA

"Thalia!" Malva hissed in a whisper, drawing me out of my distracted musings. The eleven-year-old rolled her eyes at me as I startled and pressed a hand to my chest. "Are you living in a dream today?"

"I'm sorry," I said sheepishly, a blush tinting my cheeks. "I don't know where my head is today." The night before had played in my brain on repeat since I'd managed to tuck myself safely back inside my bedroom in the early morning hours with no one the wiser that I'd ever been missing.

I alternated between heat-inducing thoughts that made me crave my stranger's touch once more, and the terror that something had gone horribly wrong. Had he somehow known I was left-handed?

It wasn't possible for him to have seen something and drawn that conclusion in our night together. To use my right hand when people were there to witness the action was deeply ingrained in me.

The only time I used my left was to draw, and even then I began with my right and shifted because I just couldn't sketch properly with my right.

I shoved the thoughts aside, knowing if there were to be some consequence for my rebellion, it would come with or without me fretting over it.

With the wedding only a month away, I intended to enjoy the limited time I was allowed with my sister before it became even harder to see her. In truth, if it hadn't been for Malva's safety hanging over my head, I would have run long ago.

Freed myself from the chains of my life and what this marriage promised to be for me. It wouldn't have mattered if I needed to take out my father's men to gain that freedom, but I couldn't risk Malva.

I couldn't take her with me, not without risking her being harmed or worse in the crossfire. Leaving her behind just was not an option, because I knew what happened when my father lost an outlet for his abuse.

My mother's death had shifted the entirety of his focus to me for the time before my stepmother came and embraced his darkness.

"Did you have a bad dream again?" she asked, concern twisting her features. It wasn't uncommon for my screams to wake the house, and for an urgent banging at my door to startle me awake. The sleep aids they made me take to prevent that usually kept the nightmares at bay.

"I just couldn't sleep is all," I said evasively. She pursed her lips, but nodded before prattling on about her day at school. I smiled through the bitterness that our lives in the same household were so vastly different. She was the treasured daughter, the one who knew no harm and could do no wrong.

Whereas I'd been born defective and punished for it every day of my life.

After my mother's death, I hadn't even been allowed to

leave for school, having private tutors brought to educate me without the corruption of outside influences. "And what did Percy do after Cassandra threw the stone at you?" I asked, humoring the crush she seemed to have on the boy she saw infrequently at the gatherings of the families. If my father ever learned of her feelings for him, even as fleeting and innocent as they were, considering they were both children, there was no telling what he would do.

"He threw it back at her and told her to stop being a nasty hag," Malva said, bright laughter tinting her sweet voice.

She was older than I'd been when my innocence was stripped away, and the mistake I'd made the night before only made me more resolved to make sure she kept that for as long as possible.

Malva could never know what a pool of blood looked like or the sounds of a blade cutting through flesh.

I'd die before I let anything stain her in the way I'd been ruined. Because in a life of misery?

She was the only thing I loved.

*If you plan to continue with this series, there's an epilogue...but I suggest you stop here if you don't like cliffhangers and don't plan to continue.*

*Thanks for reading!*

# EPILOGUE

CALIX

*One month later..*

Christian climbed into the backseat of the SUV beside me, the cane clutched tightly in his grip. He handed it over the moment the door closed and Lex pulled away from the driveway. Christian accepted the towel I handed him, wiping his blood-stained hands on it and glaring at the red caked underneath his fingernails. "Any survivors?" I asked, not bothering to take my eyes off the weapon in my hands.

By the time I finished with Origen, he'd be lucky if I hadn't shoved it so far up his ass it came out his mouth.

"Everyone who was in the house is taken care of," he said. There wasn't a hint of remorse for killing the men he'd been forced to work alongside in his time watching over Thalia, but he also didn't dare disobey my orders in the slightest.

I'd known Thalia suffered at her father's hands, but I'd never known the extent he'd gone to correct her "unsatisfactory" behavior. The whiteness of her scars made me believe that she'd had them long before I planted Christian.

That was the only reason he still breathed, because I couldn't expect him to protect her from something that had happened before his arrival. That responsibility fell on my shoulders alone.

Having him retrieve the cane had been a risk. If anyone in the Karras Estate had managed to contact someone, my plans would go out the window quickly. But I couldn't explain the need for the cane, beyond the need to get Thalia the revenge she so desperately deserved.

And that cane would be a part of it.

"The church?" Lex asked from the front.

"Yes. Is everyone ready and waiting?" I asked, holding his gaze in the rearview mirror.

"All are in position," Rafael said, turning to look back at me. "You ready for this? For her to know who you are?"

"The next time she comes on my cock, it will be my name on her lips. What do you think?" I asked, raising an eyebrow at him. Rafael chuckled, that deep, twisted laugh that made men quiver in fear.

I had no doubt he was occupied by thoughts of the girl he'd left in Chicago. Watching and waiting for her to be old enough to claim.

We pulled onto the street where the church waited. "Has it started?"

"Just about to get to the I do's," Rafael said, glancing down at his phone and the updates he received regularly from our contact inside. Not *all* of the five families had been pleased by the turn of events that had led us here twelve years ago.

I nodded as the SUV pulled up directly in front of the church, watching as my men poured out of the vehicles lining the street and emerged from alleys.

By the time we were done, the church would be bathed in the blood of everyone Thalia knew.

And she would be my wife.

*Thalia*

I was going to die. If my heart didn't give out and my body didn't crumple to the floor in a pile of flesh and blood right there at the altar, Damianos would kill me when he realized I wasn't a virgin. My stranger's somehow intimate knowledge that I was left-handed naturally left me feeling like I'd walked into a trap. Like this entire thing was a stage, and I'd end up in the pits where my mother had died.

I couldn't even look at the man next to me, and he was about to be my husband. Only minutes separated me from being Thalia Hasapis, and his dark eyes were inquisitive as he stared at me from his peripheral vision. The Priest continued with his rambling rant as if anyone cared about God's wishes when I was in a church filled with murderers and thieves.

"Do you, Thalia, take Damianos to be your lawfully wedded husband?" The room seemed to vibrate around me, a buzzing sound filling my ears as I tried to process the words I'd known were coming. Still, I went rigid. My world ended, narrowing down to the memory of a stranger's hands on me, of his mouth and his body against mine.

Did I take the man I never wanted? I didn't know if I

could live my life knowing that real passion was out there, but never being able to reach out and grab it for myself.

My mouth dropped open to answer, the only words I could ever truly give in the situation. The choice had been taken from me before I'd even known what marriage was. The name and the face of my husband was irrelevant.

The result would be the same.

I should just be grateful that he didn't appear to be an overly cruel man. He had high expectations of me, but he wasn't the same kind of monster as my father. He'd be a step up from my life at home.

Of all the men who might have won the right to marry me in ο λάκκος, Damianos was arguably the best of my choices. Even still, I couldn't make my lips form the words.

Damianos clenched his jaw as he watched my reaction, his anger palpable in the air as he waited. I knew every second of hesitation was an embarrassment that I would likely suffer for, both from my soon-to-be husband and my father. His hand tightened on mine as he turned me to face him, his face transforming with a brief understanding. "I will protect you, η νύφη μου."

I raised my eyes to his finally, my heart filling with a moment of hope. Perhaps he wouldn't kill me when he discovered the truth. "I—"

My voice cut off as a scream tore through the chapel, and I craned my neck to face the door. Something hot and wet splashed against my cheek, and I nearly fell to my knees as Damianos dropped to the floor. His grip on my hand tried to drag me down with him, and I gasped as his head struck against the wood floor. The gaping hole where his eye had once been stared back at me, his other staring up blankly and unseeing.

Prying my fingers free desperately, I reached up to wipe

the wetness from my face. They came away stained with dark fluid, thick and viscous. I'd seen enough of it, felt enough of it on my skin to know exactly what it was.

*Blood.*

The blood of the man who should have been my husband. I spun to face the doorway and the crowd of men filling the back of the chapel with assault weapons in their grips, but it wasn't the crowd and impending death that stole the breath from my lungs.

It was the shockingly familiar face tucked just behind the barrel of a pistol with a silencer attached to the front. The light eyes that studied me intently, cold and unyielding. No trace of the teasing amusement or dominant lover I'd met a month before remained, but there was no doubt that they were one and the same.

Damianos' mother screamed, lunging to her feet in the audience and drawing my eyes to her finally and away from the man I'd never thought to see again. Her chest shook as my stranger turned his gun to her, firing two shots into her chest. Inky black bloomed on the fabric of her dress as she staggered and then fell to the floor, the rest of the people in the chapel finally vaulting to their feet in panic.

Jeno and my father pulled out their own weapons as the five families erupted into chaos and bullets exploded everywhere. Despite the gunfire, the stranger from the hotel lowered his gun and stalked up the center aisle toward me. His eyes never left mine, leaving no doubt to his intent as the lightness in them shone with fury.

I darted forward, snatching Malva's hand in mine and yanking her away from her mother where she huddled in the pews. She cowered, clinging to me as I lifted the side of my dress and ran for the door at the back of the chapel. The

Priest ran in front of us, leaving the people of his congregation to their fate as he saved himself.

I supposed my father's donations meant nothing once he was dead.

Just as we reached the door, a familiar grunt sounded behind us. I spun, looking to confirm the sound I would never forget. Even when we'd been children, the sound of him when he was hurt had been imprinted on my memory in a time when I'd wanted nothing more than for him to love me as a brother should. But he hadn't, and he'd deserved every bit of punishment he got.

Jeno's eyes widened as he touched the wound in his chest. A knife protruded from it, my stranger staring him down as he pulled the knife free.

"Run, Thalia," Jeno begged, his voice rasping out his final breath as he collapsed to the floor. My stepmother's scream echoed behind me, her body curled over my father where he sat clutching his side while the stranger stalked toward me.

I shoved a sobbing Malva forward, fleeing from the chapel and into the back. Down the hall, to the right. We moved as quickly as we could. The door at the back loomed large and welcoming, the Priest's hand only inches from grasping the knob as he turned back to speak to us urgently. "My car is back here," Father Yiannis said. I had no faith in his desire or interest to keep us safe, but if we could just get away from the massacre then maybe there would be hope.

The back door opened in, two men stepping into the church and staring us down as they closed the door behind him. I came to a stop, backing away a step as they walked closer. "Miss Karras, I have to ask that you and your sister return to the wedding," one of them said, his lips tipping up in amusement.

"What wedding?" I hissed, shoving Malva behind me. "They killed the groom!"

"There will still be a wedding, λουλούδι μου" a voice behind me said. *My flower.* My blood froze, turning to solid ice in my veins as I spun around slowly. The voice was familiar, the same raspy one that had murmured orders to me while I writhed beneath him.

His face was the same, breathtaking and rugged in a way I didn't often see with the proper men of the five families.

But that name? That name was something from the past. A ghost who had left me to the fate my family had chosen when I'd been too young to understand he wouldn't come back for me.

And all that he'd left me to suffer.

As soon as my eyes connected with his light gray stare, I wondered how I hadn't seen it. Calix had been my protector. My everything.

An arrogant smirk twisted his lips as he watched the breath expel from my lungs in sudden shock.

"Hello, Little One."

The end for now

Continue the Massacred Dreams series in book one, Dreams of the Deadly, coming soon.
www.adelaideforrest.com

New to Adelaide Forrest's Bellandi World Syndicate?

You can find Rafael & Isa's story in the Beauty in Lies series (now complete).
Start with Until Tomorrow Comes.

Go back to the beginning with Matteo & Ivory's story in Bloodied Hands.

Newsletter
https://www.subscribepage.com/k7v4k1

## ALSO BY ADELAIDE FORREST

### Bellandi World Syndicate Universe

**Bellandi Crime Syndicate Series**

Bloodied Hands

Forgivable Sins

Grieved Loss

Shielded Wrongs

Scarred Regrets - Coming Soon

**Massacred Dreams Series**

Dreams of the Vengeful

**Beauty in Lies Series**

Until Tomorrow Comes

Until Forever Ends

Until Retribution Burns

Until Death Do Us Part

### Other Dark Romance

**Black Heart Romance Presents Heaven & Hell**

Wrong - Coming December 3, 2021

### Romantic Suspense Novellas

**The Men of Mount Awe Series**

Deliver Me from Evil

**Kings of Conquest - Cowritten with Lyric Cox**

Claiming His Princess

Stealing His Princess

Printed in Great Britain
by Amazon

70299431R00066